**NEW YORK REVIEW BOOKS**
CLASSICS

T0017472

# THE WOUNDED AGE *and* EASTERN TALES

FERIT EDGÜ (b. 1936) is the author of more than forty books of prose, poetry, essays, and art criticism. He received his fine arts education in Germany and France. In 1976, he founded Ada Press, an important publishing venue for contemporary Turkish and international poetry. The press remained active until 1990. A member of the '50s Circle of writers that included some of the most innovative modern Turkish voices, Edgü has had a transformative role in the development of Turkish short fiction. His short-story collection *Bir Gemide* (In a Ship) received the 1979 Sait Faik Prize, and his novel *Eylülün Gölgesinde Bir Yaz* (A Summer in September's Shade) received the Sedat Simavi Literary Prize in 1988. *Hakkari'de Bir Mevsim* (A Season in Hakkari), considered his masterpiece, was made into a movie and received several awards at the 1983 Berlin International Film Festival. His work has been translated into several languages, including French, German, Italian, and Japanese, and his novel *Noone* (*Kimse*) is available in English, in Fulya Peker's translation.

ARON AJI, the director of translation programs at the University of Iowa, is a native of Turkey and has translated works by modern and contemporary Turkish writers, including Bilge Karasu, Elif Shafak, Latife Tekin, Murathan Mungan, and Ferit Edgü. His Karasu translations include *Death in Troy*; *The Garden of Departed Cats*, which received the 2004 National Translation Award; and *A Long Day's Evening*, which was a finalist for the 2013 PEN Translation Prize. Aji was president of the American Literary Translators Association from 2016 to 2019. He is co-translator with David Gramling of Mungan's *Valor: Stories*, which was awarded the 2021 Global Humanities Translation Prize.

# THE WOUNDED AGE *and* EASTERN TALES

FERIT EDGÜ

*Translated from the Turkish and with an afterword by*
ARON AJI

NEW YORK REVIEW BOOKS

*New York*

THIS IS A NEW YORK REVIEW BOOK
PUBLISHED BY THE NEW YORK REVIEW OF BOOKS
435 Hudson Street, New York, NY 10014
www.nyrb.com

*Eastern Tales* was first published by Yapı Kredi Yayınları as *Doğu Öyküleri* in 1995;
*The Wounded Age* was published by Can Yayınları as *Yaralı Zaman* in 2007.

Excerpts from Anton Chekhov's *The Steppe*, translated from the Russian by
Constance Garnett, 1888.

Library of Congress Cataloging-in-Publication Data
Names: Edgü, Ferit, 1936– author. | Aji, Aron, 1960– translator, writer of
    afterword. | Edgü, Ferit, 1936– Yaralı zaman. English. | Edgü, Ferit, 1936–
    Doğu öyküleri. English.
Title: The wounded age and Eastern tales / by Ferit Edgü ; translated from the
    Turkish by Aron Aji; afterword by Aron Aji.
Other titles: Eastern tales
Description: New York: New York Review Books, [2022] | Series: New York
    Review Books classics
Identifiers: LCCN 2022010796 (print) | LCCN 2022010797 (ebook) |
    ISBN 9781681376769 (paperback) | ISBN 9781681376776 (ebook)
Subjects: LCGFT: Prose poems.
Classification: LCC PL248.E3 W68 2022 (print) | LCC PL248.E3 (ebook) |
    DDC 894/.3513—dc23/eng/20220526
LC record available at https://lccn.loc.gov/2022010796
LC ebook record available at https://lccn.loc.gov/2022010797

ISBN 978-1-68137-676-9
Available as an electronic book; ISBN 978-1-68137-677-6

Printed in the United States of America on acid-free paper.
10  9  8  7  6  5  4  3  2  1

# CONTENTS

# THE WOUNDED AGE

The wounded body, the wounded land,
The wounded age—

—GEORGE SEFERIS, *Merés* (Days)

*What's wrong, the Woman says.*
*Nothing, the Man says. Nothing.*
*You're here but it's like you're not, she says.*
*I'm leaving soon, he says.*
*Where, she asks.*
*East. The mountains.*
*She puts down her fork.*
*I expected that.*
*The Man is silent.*
*The Woman asks, Why?*
*The newspaper is sending me.*
*They couldn't find anyone else to send there?*
*I asked for the assignment, he says.*
*To see it in the flesh again? she asks.*
*A bitter smile in her eyes.*
*Maybe.*
*Missed the mountains, haven't you?*
*Maybe.*
*And the people, you must've missed them, too.*
*The Man is silent.*
*People who kill each other.*
*The Man is silent.*
*And you think you can stop the bloodletting?*
*No, he says.*
*Why then?*
*To go, he says.*

*But you already did.*
*That was long ago.*
*Nothing changes, she says.*
*We'll see.*
*You want to see the dead? Are you going there to bury them?*
*The Man is silent.*
*I am full, she says, leaving the table.*
*Turn off the television, he says.*
*She turns it off.*
*Would you like a drink?*
*She gets up without waiting for an answer, prepares a drink.*
*Handing him the glass: Is this our last night together?*
*Yes.*
*Then let's reminisce, she says, let's talk.*
*You don't regret looking back.*
*They are silent.*
*The Woman already lost in memories.*
*Remember the town by the lake? she asks.*
*The lakeside hotel, he says, years ago.*
*Yes, you traveled south, I traveled north.*
*True, I traveled south, he says.*
*We hiked the mountains around the lake.*
*I remember.*
*The Woman smiles.*
*But those were different mountains.*
*I haven't forgotten.*
*Surely not. You worried about an avalanche when I screamed.*
*The Man smiles.*
*They are silent. Sipping their drinks. Taking a drag or two on*
*their cigarettes.*
*They are silent.*
*She gets up to refill her glass. Will you describe one last time*
*the night by that lake?*
*She leaves the room and returns wearing a silk robe. Kneeling*

down in front of him, she first removes his shirt. Then his shoes. His socks. His trousers. She burrows her head in his lap. His hands caress her hair. In a barely audible voice, he describes the night they spent in that lakeside town, after a long absence. Just words. No sentences. Then he falls silent. I must be somewhere else, he thinks. Must be dreaming. But who's this person lying on me? This hair? This deep, dark, tenacious well trying to draw me in? He opens his eyes for a moment: A mountain deer leaping among the ceiling beams. Then a second one, then a third . . .

A hallucination, the Man thinks.

He doesn't want to close his eyes.

Just watches.

Then more deer, running, chasing, being chased.

After wandering among the peaks, he suddenly steps off a precipice. Falling, he screams.

Herds of mountain deer running, wave after wave across the ceiling that is now a forest.

What happened, the Woman asks.

Don't you see? the Man says.

Her eyes turn toward the ceiling, Yes, she says, I see.

Those are mountain deer.

Mountain deer, yes. Roe deer, gazelles, wild goats . . .

Is this an illusion?

No, she says. Since I too can see them.

What is it, then?

We're sending you off, this is our farewell. Now close your eyes and don't open them until I say so.

The Man closes his eyes.

For a long time. The man has another dream.

Open your eyes, a voice says.

He opens his eyes: Mountains.

Who made you come? It's not safe here.
It's been snowing for seven days.
It sure has.
Wolves are coming down.
They sure will.
Gunshots at night.
Sure you'll hear them.
Watch your step. Don't stand in the way of bullets,
watch out for wolves or vultures. We need you.
For the first time someone was talking to me like this.
Blizzard. Blinding.
I buried myself inside my coat.
My eyelids felt heavy, but I tried to not fall asleep.
I wouldn't wake up if I did.
We need you.
Who needs me—
Who needs whom on these mountains, in this freezing hell?
I removed my hat.
The blizzard stopped. Surrounding me, five or six children.
I tried to smile.
They smiled back.
Where you coming from?
Where are you going?
*Ji vir û pê de rê nîn e.*
*Qey tu nizanî?*
There's no road beyond here.
Don't you know?
There was strong tea. *Yufka* and herbed cheese.
I took a sip of the bitter tea.

Someone held me by the hand and walked me to a house.
Later, a deep, warm darkness.
*Nexêr, tarîyeke mîna qeşayê.*
*Reştarî.*
No, a bone-chilling darkness.
Pitch-black.

We're passing through settlements, sprawled out, random.
In the distance, lost among the rocks, villages, hamlets,
encampments.
As if oblivious to each other.
Barely any roads in sight. And the few we can see separate
more than connect the villages, hamlets, encampments.
A dirt path—unclear where it starts or where it ends.
Another path descending to the water. A third, curving
around a hill.
Like a labyrinth. Then. Nothing. A tree here, a tree there.
Why aren't they closer? Why do they live scattered like this?
People here, Vahap says, don't like living too close together.
Up on the mountain, say, by a stream, you'd see a house.
More like a burrow. You'd think maybe it's a stable.
Push open the door and go in.
A woman waiting for her man greets you.
Inside is dark, like it's twilight.
In winter, sooty, full of smoke.
In a corner, you hear the cries of a baby you can't make out.
Another baby crawls through the dark, finds your feet, wraps
herself around them. In those small hands clutching your
legs, you sense some kind of pleading: Don't hurt us. Spare
us. We, here...
Leaning against a rock, staring at a sheep pen, he's telling
me all this—Vahap, my guide.
If you'd like, let's stop by, open the door, and go in, he says.
I turn away.
No need, I say. Even if I don't see it, what you say must be

true. One can't make up these sorts of stories. Besides, I suspect we'll see worse things.

We stop at a bridge.

Getting out of the jeep, I approach the Lieutenant who's guarding the bridge.

After introductions, I gesture toward the people gathered on the other end.

Can I talk to them?

Do you know their language?

No.

Then how will you? They don't know your language either.

My guide's with me, I say, pointing at Vahap, who is sitting on the back of the jeep.

The Lieutenant scans Vahap.

Talk then, he says. But only with those who are on this end of the bridge. The ones on the other end—not allowed.

Driving down a deserted road. No one. Just the jinn playing ball, as they say.

Aren't there outlaws around? I ask my guide.

The reply comes from the driver.

Don't be afraid, Bey, those you call outlaws don't come down this far. Even if they did, they wouldn't ambush you here.

The outlaws stay in the mountains, Vahap adds.

Good that we didn't bring rifles, I say.

True, Vahap agrees.

The driver: Not much to hunt around here, besides.

Even if there were, who'd dare . . .

Vahap completes the driver's thought: God forbid!

They come in wave after wave. Down the mountains, down the rocks.

Women, men, children. A human deluge.

Some carrying saddlebags. Others, rifles. Their women and children on mules. Or their wounded.

Not their dead. Those, they've buried.

The Captain standing next to me opens his hands out. So many of them, he says. Open the border, they said, we opened it. And what if we didn't? They'd still come. Where else would they go?

A human deluge. The closer they get, the more we see their anguish.

Doomsday, I murmur to myself.

You haven't seen doomsday yet, Vahap says.

As if our own troubles weren't enough, the Captain says.

Don't mind it, Commander, I say. Two troubles are no worse than one.

The Captain looks at me, puzzled.

I light a cigarette and offer him one.

I didn't quite get what you meant, the Captain says, lighting his cigarette.

To be honest, neither did I, I say.

Nor did I, Vahap says.

They've been settled in a camp.

Access granted, we enter the grounds.

The photographer, flustered, runs around taking pictures.

A woman approaches us.

Write about me too, she says. Tell him to take my picture.

I ask for her name.

Besna, she tells Vahap, Tell him my children's names too.

Azad, Behrem, Zuhan, Lokman, Salih, Keve, Melek, Yusuf, Veysel, Ferman . . .

*Çavani*? I ask her how she's doing.

And where did you learn that word, Vahap asks.

From them, I say.

Azad and Zuhan are here, Vahap says, she doesn't know where the others are.

Let's see what else you'll learn around these mountains.

I ask the first villager I meet: How was the journey?

The villager understands nothing. Rubbing his beard, *Alaikumselâm*, he says.

I turn to my guide. Ask him, I say.

What shall I ask him, Vahap says.

Ask him how was his journey.

How would it be, he says. It was bad. It was no journey, leaving their land, their home.

I didn't ask you, I asked him. Ask him. How long since they left?

Vahap says something then something else to the old man. The old man looks like he's counting.

He lifts his head, stares at the hills along the border and talks, as if talking to them.

Translate, I say.

Six months, he says, it's been six months.

The old man keeps talking to the hills.

What else is he saying?

He lost a son in the mountains, Vahap says. Couldn't find his body.

The old man is now sobbing as he talks.

He kicks the ground. Picks up stones, hurls them at the border.

Vahap says, He's asking why the young must die while the old keep living.

Ask him where they'll go now.

Vahap talks to the old man.

Wherever they tell him to go, he says.

Vahap.

What's your name, I ask the child standing alone on the side of the road, staring at the hill.

Maral.

Where're you from, Maral?

Nowhere. I'm here.

What're you waiting for here?

My Aga, my father.

And where is your Aga?

She gestures toward the mountain: Up there.

How many days have you been here, Maral?

Many.

How do you know your Aga will come?

Everyone's coming. He'll come too.

If he comes, he'll find you in the village. Let's take you there.

She shakes her head. Then she starts screaming.

There, see, he is coming! Didn't I tell you! He is coming!

We look in the direction she is looking.

Empty. We see nothing.

Where, Maral, I ask.

She points at the summit.

There. Up there. Look, look, he is coming down.

I look at Vahap.

Yes, I see, he says, there, he's coming down.

I told you, Maral says.

She's dreaming, Vahap says. Let's keep going.

The voice echoing in the mountains:

*Surrender the refugees...gees...gees... to the stadium...
ium...ium... in Bilbili...li...li... district...trict...
trict... During searches...earches...earches... residents...
dents...dents... found...ound...ound... to harbor...
arbor...arbor... refugees...gees...gees... in their homes...
omes...omes...will be prosecuted...cuted...cuted...*

A peasant standing next to us.

What's it saying, he asks.

Vahap summarizes the words echoing in the mountains.

Am I to turn in my brothers who crossed the border? the peasant asks.

He hasn't even had a morsel to eat. Isn't my home my brother's home?

Shaking his head, Allah, Allah, he says and walks away.

Some days don't end, Vahap told me.

They last longer than weeks, even months. Sunset's so long in coming that you think time's stopped. Damned day, you say, does it never end? No, it doesn't, it doesn't end.

Some days are long like this. Others a whole lot shorter.

You look up, the sun's up. You look down, it's set. What've I got done, you ask yourself. Nothing. But, to be honest, I've not seen too many short days. I've seen many endless days and as many endless nights. Nights full of restless nightmares, visions real as real.

People who age in one day, their hair turns white overnight— you must've known some of them, too.

The days here, never mind what people say, they're always long.

Summer's also long. And winter. Days and nights, endless.

The yarn you're spinning, I told Vahap. All in all, we've been here just two days. Maybe we'll get the permit tomorrow and drive out.

I'm not thinking about the permit, Vahap said. I don't need no permit. I go anywhere I want, anytime I care to. I'm trying to tell you about time. Time here. I imagined a stranger like you would find it useful.

I looked at the mountains, the sharp cliffs, the peaks covered with clouds. I suddenly felt a cold wind. In my marrow.

No one can describe time, I said. Look at you, standing there, talking nonsense.

The mountains separated them, says Vahap, my guide.
Half here, the other half there.
Half of what, I ask.
Half of everyone, of everything, Vahap says. Just about.
Villages, families, tribes.
This way, they are united, I say.
How so, Vahap asks. People here have barely enough to feed
their own children.
A villager comes by. Greeting us, he asks, Why are you here?
To Vahap, Don't you know they're bombing the mountains?
What if they drop one here? What business do you have
being here? There's no life here. Only death. What business
do you have being here?
He takes a cigarette from Vahap, then walks away.
Do you know him, I ask Vahap.
My uncle, says Vahap. One of my thousand uncles.

They escaped with their animals.

Not just horses or mules. Sheep as well, thirty, forty of them.

Most perished on the way, a man says.

He's not crying. Maybe smiling.

They carried two of the wounded sheep on their shoulders.

He gestures at the big cauldron nearby: Now they're both in there.

A woman is standing by the boiling cauldron.

Her belly up to her nose.

She uncovers the cauldron, stirs.

A pungent meat smell.

Fate is fate. Born this side of the mountain or the other, makes no difference for the baby.

Is that what she says, I ask Vahap.

Yes, that's what she says.

And that she'll name the baby, Ferman—decree.

It's this land's custom, Vahap says.

Ferman's the child born in exile.

Then he adds: They want us to join them for dinner.

I'm sitting on a rock, notebook in hand, taking notes.

A man approaches me, stops, and looks.

I stop writing and look at him too.

Can you write a letter for me, Bey? he asks.

I can, I say. Let me hear it.

Write then, he says, that I've never forgotten her. That she's never left my dreams. Did you write?

I wrote.

Write then: We crossed the mountains, made it here safely. But who knows where we'll be sent next. Did you write?

I wrote.

I'll send word to you when I get there. So you come and find me. Or I, you. Did you write?

I wrote.

That's all, he says. Now hand me the letter.

I tear out the page; handing it to him, I ask, And to whom did we write the letter?

She knows who she is, he says.

Folding the paper in quarters, he puts it in his pocket.

All well and good, but how are you going to get it to her?

Eh, I'll maybe find someone headed that way.

Flashlight in hand, I'm walking around.
Children, covered with blankets, lying asleep.
Women unseen.
Men wander about, in fours and fives.
Cigarettes between their lips flicker like fireflies in the night.
They're speaking softly; I can't understand a word.
Just a soft murmur.
My light falls upon a woman breastfeeding her baby.
She's holding the baby with one hand, her breast with the other.
Her startled gaze caught in the light. No shame. Just fear.
She lowers her head, over her baby.
I turn my flashlight in another direction.
A tap on my shoulder. I turn. Someone else with a flashlight.
He asks, Are you looking for someone?
No one, I say. No one. Or everyone.
It's nighttime, stranger, go and sleep, says the man with the flashlight.
I feel like a hunter lost in a forest or on some mountain—here, surrounded by these people—like I'd been chasing a prey that led me wherever it wished, like I'd lost its tracks and now I can't tell where I am or where I came from.
You should leave, the man says, pointing the flashlight at the darkness. Walk straight and you'll be out.
Thank you, I say.
I showed you the way, he says. The rest is up to you. Go now. Goodbye.

Would they jail us here, one of them asks.

Why would they jail you, I say.

'Cause we crossed the border.

You've been crossing the border all these years, I say.

That was then, says the other.

No one's jailing anyone. You're in your country here.

What did you say, Vahap asks.

That they shouldn't be afraid. Tell them, I say.

Who can live on these mountains without fear, Bey? Vahap asks.

You may be right, Vahap, but you can't live with fear either.

The two mountain men laugh, as if they understand what we're saying.

Night.

A song takes wing, a *türkü*.

A woman's voice.

It's more than a song—a wailing, a grievance.

Where's this *türkü* from, what part of the country, I ask.

It's not a *türkü*, it's an elegy, Vahap says.

What's it saying?

They must've just come up with it, it's new to me.

He listens to the elegy sounding through the night.

Then, after a long silence, Vahap translates. I've known mountains, but not exile, she says. The night—a dagger in my heart, she says. Who's my foe, I can't tell. Pull the dagger out, she says. Come, pull the dagger out. My blood . . .

You can stop, I say. I know that elegy.

I doubt that, Vahap says. Even I haven't heard it.

Your elegies are all the same, I say, raising my voice.

Every one of them, the same.

Then, maybe to make amends, to win his heart back.

Like death, I say.

Dark shadows stir in the dark.

I call Vahap.

The shadows stop. Briefly. Then one of them approaches.

You called me? he asks.

The voice is not Vahap's voice.

I called Vahap, I say.

I'm Vahap, says the voice in the dark.

I pull out my cigarette lighter and light it, hold it toward his face.

A bearded, old, tired face.

You're not the Vahap I called, I say.

Then give me a cigarette and I'll leave, he says.

I've long been waiting here for someone like you.

Night.

They're gathered around the fire.

I'm in a corner, as if to hide, smoking, listening to them.

Where we going tomorrow, one asks.

Staying here still, the one next to him says.

And the day after tomorrow?

Here still.

Well, we won't be here forever, says the first one.

Word is, we're in our father's home, another one says.

And where is my father's home?

*Ne bilem, ne bilem, ne bilem.*

Don't know, don't know, don't know.

Accursed fate! says the man sitting across.

Then, an old woman: We're alive, aren't we? Be thankful.

Vahap translates, I write it in my head.

Then they emerged from the night.
Crawling, crawling on the ground.
Hurtling against rocks.
They emerged from the night.
One by one by one.
Each calling out his own name.
For each had a name.
And each one named crossed the border, went inside.
Picked up a rifle.
Returned to the night.


Then they emerged from the water.
Bone-chilling water. They emerged.
Outside, bone-chilling air.
One by one by one.
Each calling out his family name.
For each had a family.
Each one named crossed the border, came outside.
Each with a rifle.
No one asked, Why?


Then they crossed into hell.
It was hell. Fire. On all sides.
They killed everyone they could find.
Killed the children. Killed the women.
The babies. The sheep. The yearling lambs.
The wolves. The dogs.

But no men. Not a man in sight.
They killed the grass. They killed the rocks.
The fields. The trees.
They killed the night and the day.


It was hell.
They didn't know whether they'd escape or where.
They just killed. Without knowing whom they killed.
Just to kill.
The mountain snow turned into blood.
The Great Zab turned into a scarlet river.
Blinding the eye that saw.
Deafening the ear that heard.
He who remembered lost his tongue.
The pencil that wrote it down broke.

We're advancing.
Along the way, only military jeeps.
Only armed soldiers.
A low-flying helicopter from time to time.
To the left, the border, its stone markers.
Beyond the border, desolation. Not a soul nor a jinn.
Suddenly, we spot a crowd by the stream, a commotion.
Women washing clothes.
Clean garments laid out to dry on the gravel, on the grass.
Not a man in sight.
Only women and children.
You should've taken their picture, Vahap says.
I did, I say.

Daybreak.

I'm watching women washing clothes by the water.

Their hands purr-purple.

I notice a bird in the brush. A kind I hadn't seen before. It turns its head, looks back, tail fluttering. The women are also watching the bird, chuckling among themselves.

I walk down, offer each woman an orange, without speaking to them.

They tuck the gifts in their bosoms, without speaking to me.

For their children, Vahap says.

Should've given the children something to eat.

Why, he asks.

So they wouldn't die hungry, I say.

Let's not kid ourselves, he says. Haven't you figured it out yet? What we got here is not a problem of conscience.

I hold the binoculars and focus. On the slopes across, wolves. I hadn't seen anything like this. A wolf pack, ten or twelve wolves, chasing a deer. A lone deer. Frantic, unsure of where to run, dashing right and left, eyes startled, anxious.

The deer seems like he's coming in my direction. I leave my hiding spot behind a rock, lower my binoculars, and reach for my rifle. My mouth parched dry. I glance down, by my feet, as if looking for a dog. There's no dog. Vahap already has his rifle aimed. Shoot, he says. Hold, I say. Wait a while. But before too long, one of the wolves catches up with the deer, leaps to latch on to his neck, but the deer, jerking back, jabs his antlers into the wolf's ribs, and starts again, escaping, tracing zigzags in the air.

The wolves appear confused.

I look through the binoculars and see blood tracks on the snow.

I'll shoot, Vahap says.

I let go of the binoculars and reach for my rifle again. Steadying it against my shoulder, I now watch through the scope, the wolves and the deer. The deer and the wolves. A sudden gunshot. But Vahap misses. *Karavana*, I say. Then I pull the trigger. The lead wolf rears up, falls to the ground. The other wolves scatter but quickly regroup. The deer, having stopped ever so briefly, springs forth running. Toward the precipice. On the edge, the deer stops. Turns his head back, sees the wolves closing in. Then, the deer falls. Down the precipice.

I freeze.

The wolves reach the edge, lean out, and see the deer lying

on the rocks. They jerk and twitch restlessly. Kick up the snow. But not one of them dares to climb down to claim the trophy.

I lower my gun, look at Vahap. He shrugs, but helplessly. Leaning his rifle against the rock, he pulls his tobacco pouch from his chest, rolls a cigarette, hands it to me, then rolls one for himself.

That's how much life he had, I suppose, Vahap says.

Not if I had a machine gun, I say, he would've lived longer.

Or:

You've no chance to save him. You pick up the binoculars and look again. The deer is panting. A second wolf catches up, claws at him. But this time the deer doesn't fall. He stands at the very edge of the precipice that separates you from them (the deer and the wolves), turns to look just for a second, and seeing the pack of hungry wolves at his back, the deer jumps off, into the emptiness, down the snow-covered rocks, crashing against these rocks, while you watch what is the first and undoubtedly only time you will see in your hunting life an act of suicide.

When the wolves reach the edge of the precipice, they stop. You keep watching. The wolves, bewildered, stare at the bottom, at the broken body of the deer, his blood on every snow-covered rock he hit along the way.

One or two of them attempt to climb down but, quickly realizing they won't succeed, return to the pack that's been watching.

That's when you regret not having a machine gun. Perhaps with a feeling of vengeance. No, not perhaps. That's what it is. A feeling that a hunter, a real hunter, should never experience.

You point the binoculars down, from the wolves down toward the dead deer. His neck is broken. His antlers shattered. Then you see his eyes. Both of them wide open. Like he's gazing at the sky.

Hunched, I'm adrift in thoughts, my left hand pressed against my cheek.

I've wandered so far that if someone came and touched me, I would fall off the cliff.

What's he staring at, I hear a crackling voice.

I turn my head in the direction of the voice. A child.

I try to smile.

He's looking at me, puzzled.

I turn away, staring again at the emptiness before me, at the steep rocks, the stream down below.

At this altitude, we don't even hear the rush, water beating against the rocks and swirling in eddies.

But I'm all ears and try to listen to the sounds rising from the moist earth, the moss-covered rocks, the dry grass.

The child points at the opposite cliff. Look, he says, prey.

I pick up my binoculars and look. Then I hand them to the child.

He asks, Don't you have a rifle?

I don't, I say.

*Mirov qet bêtiving diçe nêçîrê?*

Who goes hunting without a rifle?

I stand up, reeling.

Dizzy.

Let's go, I tell him, lead the way.

A horse tied to a rock.

Who is there, I ask.

No one, the child says.

Were you following me, I ask.

*Min hespê xwe ji tere anîye.*

I brought you my horse.
I get up from the rock I had been sitting on.
I aim my camera at this little man holding the stirrup, looking at me.
What had I come searching for that this child came and found me?


*Te xezalek kuşt.*
*Wê xwedajê min ê Mezin bi xezalekê te bikuje.*
You hunt the gazelle.
My Almighty hunts you with the gazelle.

It's time I left this place, freed myself.

I've felt like I was called here for a reason. A particular hunt. Or a trap. For whom it is set, I don't know, but I sense its presence.

I need to think harder: What is it, after all these years, that reawakens in me the urge to hunt?

I had quit, laid down the rifle for good: Why has this urge, long dead, suddenly come alive? Who brought it back to life? Who handed me the rifle? Who introduced me to this writer?

Why, how, do I find myself caught up in these events? Made to witness them?

I'd been living my small life. What's changed me?

The mountains.

The mountains and the people.

No, only the mountains.

Don't come back before you see Zab, they'd told me.

I saw the river at last.

Exactly three days before my return date.

I was walking—alone, no rifle, no dog.

On a sunny day when the melting snow was rushing down like mountain streams.

Boots on, gaiters wrapped around my legs, sheepskin cloak on my shoulders, keffiyeh on my head, I had walked quite far from the city, to a spot where the river reached a clearing. As if I wanted the extraordinary sight to be etched in my memory. I looked: A boat in the distance, or a raft, or maybe a canoe. An old man in it. He wasn't sculling. He was pulling in a net. Approaching the riverbank. Thinking I might help, I veered down toward where the boat—or raft or canoe or whatever—was approaching. Once there, I stopped and shouted. But the old fisherman waved his hand, waving me away. Me? I looked around, there was no one else. I waved my arms and shouted again. (Now I could see him better—his white beard, crooked back, the wide-mesh net he had cast on the shallow water and was now struggling to retrieve.) His every move seemed like an exertion, probably because of age.

As the boat came closer, his gestures became more discernible. But I had no intention of leaving. There were a pair of hip waders lying on the rocks; I put them on, plunged into the water, and walked toward the boat. The old man started yelling in a language I didn't understand, while he kept trying to retrieve the net. We got closer and closer to each other, and soon I realized why the old man was struggling to pull the net onto his boat: There were no fish; the net was filled with corpses of women, men, and children.

This time, I screamed. The old man, still holding on to the net, straightened his body, and, passing the net to his left hand, wiped his sweaty brow with his right hand. I told you to leave, he yelled, this time in my language. Now leave, you saw what you wanted to see. Go the hell away. I started walking backward to the edge, my eyes still fixed on him. Corpses of women, of children, swept in the current, brushed past my legs. I screamed. When I came to, my heart pounding against its shell, I was sure I woke up in the afterworld.


Close to noon, I arrived at the door of Sheik Abdullah to ask him to interpret my dream. He didn't look surprised in the least when he saw me standing before him. He let me in. After offering me tea, he listened to my dream. He remained quiet for a while, pensive. Then he got up from his cushion, walked to his wooden chest, and took out a few thick, handwritten leather-bound books. He read. Exhaled. He read. Exhaled. He came back, holding an unlit candle. Your dream cannot be interpreted, he said. You saw Zab in your dream and saw it exactly as it is.

He handed me the candle.

Take it, light it when you find yourself in darkness.

Noticing that I understood nothing, he added:

We couldn't interpret your dream, but at least, for a brief spell, we should illuminate your night.

When I touched the candle, I understood the real meaning of my dream: To give out light, the object, or the self, consumed in the burning flame . . .

I got up to leave. Our eyes met. As if ashamed, the Sheik Effendi turned his gaze away, looking at the ceiling, the walls, the floor. Contrary to custom, he didn't let me kiss his hand.

Morning fog. I am watching the water in the distance.
I light a cigarette. Raise my coat collar. Lean on my walking stick.

*Were vir! Mere dûr!*

Come here! Don't go far!

I look, there's no one by the water.

Smoke is rising off the water. As if it has a voice. I listen to my heartbeat, to the reflections of the rising sun on the rock surfaces. The river's sound overwhelms all other sounds. No dogs barking, no wolves howling. Nothing. No rifle sound. Not even a horse neighing. Nothing. Just nature. The river. The wind, like the earth inhaling.

I listen.

Then the smoke disperses. Reflections of sunlight off the rock surfaces meet the water. The water changes color, red as blood. You wanted to see it, here, see it then, I say to myself. I toss my cigarette. Leaning on my stick, I walk down the hill to the road, then, crossing it, reach the river's edge.

Startled, I see an old man sitting on his heels by the water. Perfectly still, he seems like he walked out of a fairy tale or a legend.

I approach him to say something, but he gestures to me to remain quiet.

Quiet, I stand still.

A while later, the old man begins to pull at a rope. Straining. Don't stand there, he says, come and help me.

I drop my walking stick, grab the end of the rope he hands me, and we begin to pull the heavy net teeming with fish of all sizes.

I told Vahap what happened that morning.

You must've had a dream, Vahap said. There's no fisherman around here. There's never been. We wouldn't know a fishing net if we saw one.

But we pulled it together, I said.

I told you, you had a dream, Vahap said. A morning dream.

I didn't insist. Just told him, Dreams are real, too.

They can be, Vahap said, but the reverse is not true.

He paused, then smiling, asked, Why wasn't I with you?

I don't know, I said.

Nobody guides anybody in dreams. That's why, Vahap said.

How come you don't write down what I say but you write down what you hear from others? Vahap asks.

I do write down what you say too.

No, you don't, Vahap counters, as if hurt.

I never saw you write.

I write at night.

That's true, you write at night. But what you write at night, is it what I tell you?

Part of it is, I say.

What about the other part, Vahap asks, suspiciously.

The other part is what I observe, I say.

Will everyone read what you've been writing? Vahap asks.

Not everyone, I say, smiling. Some people probably will.

Those who read it, will they know me? Vahap asks.

They most certainly will.

Good, Vahap says, then I'll keep telling you things. Otherwise, I don't want to say another word anymore.

Go to sleep, I tell him, holding my pencil. We have to wake up early tomorrow morning.

Don't talk like you don't know, he says. You know I don't sleep at night.

Then why do you close your eyes, I say.

Vahap laughs.

To fool those checking on me, he says.

Did he come here to suffer, Great Zab
He came here to find you, talk to you
He came to sow his seeds in your fields
He cast his words in the air, Great Zab, so they'd find you
His words came back empty-handed
Or are you no longer of this land, Great Zab
Or have you left a long time ago
My life begins at your wellspring, tracks your mountain
streams to the arid fields where you vanish, and no further
He who knows you and he who doesn't, can they be one and
the same
He who knows you and he who knows suffering can be one
and the same, but that's different
He who knows you and he who doesn't fear death, he who
knows neither death nor fear, they can be one and the same,
but that's different
He wants to draw hundreds of faces on your stones and send
them down your rushes
And he wants to release all his words on rafts down your
waters
This is why he is here and he wants nothing else

Where to next? Vahap asked.

Hunting, they said, so we went. Came back empty-handed. To the border, they said. What's at the border? People on both sides. Soldiers on both sides. Guns, grenades, fire on both sides.

Fear on both sides, Vahap said. What's there to see? People.

What'll we say to them?

Nothing. We'll listen. Listen to what they say.

Maybe something we don't know.

Who knows.

What'll we give them?

Nothing. We'll take their photographs. We'll welcome them.

Welcome them where?

Among us.

God, why can't people stay put?

How can they, when no one leaves them alone?

Don't cry, I tell the little girl beside me.

Don't cry, your father will come. Let's get a hot bowl of soup, come, I say.

Inside my left hand—I forgot it was hanging by my side—I sense the presence of a sweaty little hand. I hold on to it and walk toward our tent.

I know, no one's waiting for me.
If I died, my body wouldn't be returned.
"Bury me at the foot of a rock
I don't need a stone or any marker."
I haven't thought much about death.
If all that death was the price we paid for having lived, I really didn't care for it.
Here: I'd just be leaving. My bag on my shoulder, my underwear in it, a sweater, plus my pencil and notebook.
Here: I'd just be leaving one last time.
Going back to the desolate mountaintop where I was born.
To the merciless winter. The wolves. The dogs.
And a few people, if any were still left.

What are you humming about, I asked.
About the river Zab, he said.
Sing it so we can also hear, I said.
Staring at the emptiness, he began reciting in a dull voice.


(Translation)
*Tell us, Zab, where are the rocks?*
*They broke off and tumbled down the gorge.*
*Tell us, Zab, where is the gorge?*
*Snowmelt carried it to the river.*
*Tell us, Zab, where is the river?*
*It took to the fields, became a wanderer.*
*Tell us, Roads, have you seen Zab?*
*He got on a truck, moved to the cities.*
*Where are the cities, Zab?*
*Far away, in no-man's-land.*
*Where is no-man's-land, Zab?*
*Written and read in a book.*
*What do the books say of it?*
*That it rode a horse to the mountain.*
*Where is the horse now, Zab?*
*Hit the rocks, lost its horseshoes.*
*Horseshoes, horseshoes, where is your horseman?*
*Horseshoes, where is your horseman?*


He stopped. Took a sip of his tea that had grown cold.
I thought he would continue, he didn't.

Beautiful song, Vahap said, but this isn't the Zab we know. I sing of my Zab.

What's he saying, I ask Vahap.

Plain nonsense, Vahap replies. He sings a Zab song, but it's not the Zab song we know.

At these words, the man chucks his tea glass on the floor and says:

*Biqeşidin herin, careke din jî li deriyê min nedin.*

Go to hell, never knock on my door again.

I get out of the jeep.

First thing I do is turn my back to the city and look at the mountain ahead.

Sümbül Mountain.

Standing there, just as I left it.

I turn and face the city. I'm startled.

I'm surrounded by people. Huddled, standing like I am, staring at the mountain.

Now they're all staring at me.

As if we're playing a game.

Fortunately, it'll get dark soon and nothing will be visible.

Not me, not the mountain.

Not the mountain, not these people.

Not these barracks, not these soldiers.

Only a sound will remain: The howl of the wind unloosed from the mountain, blowing in our direction. A howl that'll lay siege to the city.

This (having lived through) I know.


I take my suitcase from the jeep and walk toward the hotel.

The crowd of people is still there, frozen, watching me.

Right then, a child—

As if he were waiting for someone, someone who has arrived.

He slowly approaches me.

Extending his hand, he touches the bag on my shoulder.

I look at him and smile.

His hand on the bag, What's this? he asks.

A tool, I say. Now my whole face is smiling.

A camera, I add.

Pulling his hand back, he asks, Where you coming from?

From far away. Very far away.

Istanbul? he asks.

Istanbul, but even farther away.

Where's your horse, he asks.

My horse got tired on the way.

Horses don't get tired, the child says, you come by jeep.

It's true, the horse got tired, stayed behind, I came by jeep.

You need a horse here. Tomorrow I bring you my father's horse.

You do that, I say. Unable to resist, I add, And what're we going to do with the horse?

Climb mountains, wander.

Fine, I say, we'll wander.

The child takes my hand, brings it to his forehead. His sweaty forehead.

That's enough for tonight, I say to myself.

Let's go home.

On this mountain where God left you all alone, by yourself, what dreams visit you?

Do you remember your childhood?

By the sea, there you are, in your trunks, under the scalding August sun, walking into the water, the pebbled seabed, without a whereto, mussels cutting into your soft soles, you dive in, your first breaststrokes, you're almost swimming, the panic when your feet can't touch the pebbles, your arms flailing, the clumsy strokes to get back to the shallow, bobbing and sinking, the seawater taste in your throat, the coughs, the panic you try to conceal, then (months later) the rainfall, the floodwaters, the metal shards and coins you look for along the riverbeds (with your friends), then the snowfall, the endless snowfall, the walk to school, the steaming cup of *salep* and the buttered *poğaça,* the walk back from school, sledding downhill, on your wooden satchel, then home, the slaps you receive, while wetting your pants, how you wish you were dead, how you wish you were not of this world.

Who died, I asked.

We don't know, they said.

How many? I asked

Which day? they asked.

Every day, I said. Don't they know the killers also get killed one day?

Three of the dead are children, a woman said, weeping.

And five women, a man added.

What business do we have on this mountain? I said. Let's get the hell out. Now.

We can't, my guide said. We're not done yet. Haven't seen all there is to see. Here, on this mountain, there's the living and the dead. We can't ignore them. Can't leave without counting them, naming them, taking notes, making a record.


Bullets flashing in the night's darkness.

Then the rattle of machine guns in the night's silence.

Then silence.

Here we are, someone said, in the night's blind spot.

Be quiet, said a voice. My voice.

I saw. I saw here. With my own eyes. Things I've never seen anywhere else. I saw mountains on fire. Rocks on fire. I saw trees uprooted. Roofs collapsed. I closed my eyes so as not to hear their screams. But I still heard them. Like they were my screams. Though they didn't sound like my screams. I didn't want to be here. I didn't want to see. But I saw. The end of the world. Was it the end of the world? I think it was. But not the end of life. Life outlasts the end-time. I know it. I've lived it. Before as well as now.

Is there a hunter around here?

Here? What's a hunter to hunt here? The prey hides in the forest. Here, as you can see, there's no forest, there are no trees. Is he going to hunt people?

But there's got to be prey.

Sure. Yes, animals.

Then where do they hide?

On the mountains.

On these bare mountains?

Don't you know, rocks are the trees of these mountains.

*Ma tu nizanî ku darên van çiyayan zinar in.*

Don't you know, rocks are the trees of these mountains.

You say you were born here, Vahap said. Me, I died here.
You say one can be born many times. And I say one can die
many times. Even in one day, you can die many times.
I'm one of them.
I'll tell you how, if you like.
No, don't, I said. I know everything.
You know nothing, Vahap said.
None of you know anything. You think you do. You don't
know. Maybe you know death. But there are many deaths,
worse and worse deaths. That, you don't know.
None of you. None of you.

See these mountains? Vahap says. These steep mountains, bare mountains, savage mountains, these terrible, obstinate mountains, wolves live there, dogs and humans. If you looked, you wouldn't see them, wouldn't know where they live, but if you climb the mountains, for this or that reason, they'd suddenly accost you; either they kill you or you kill them. Whoever draws faster.

(Who am I telling this to?)

Don't hope in vain, he continues.

You'll never reach the summit. No one ever has.

No one?

They say one did, but it's not known if he reached the summit. Because he never returned.

Who was it?

I don't know. Neither his name nor when he climbed the mountain, nor whom he watched with his binoculars, how high he climbed, whether he reached the top, whether he got eaten by the wolves or the dogs.

If he did make the summit, what he saw, even whether or not he lived afterward, no one knows.


What's the point of all this nonsense, I ask.

Why are you telling me these stories?

So you know, he says. Nonsense, maybe so, but that's the mountains' story.

Looking at the water spreading in all directions, I ask, What's this?

A new tributary, my guide says. It hasn't hollowed out its bed yet. In time, it will. It'll become a stream or maybe a river. It always does. Then it dries out.

Where's my mother? Where's my father? My brothers, my sisters?

Where's my dog? Where's my house? Where's my village? Where are my mountains? Where am I? Where's here?

Desolate. Eerie emptiness. But a voice kept screaming these questions.

I wanted to photograph this voice. The one asking these questions. That's why I was sent here. I could hear the voice but saw no one to whom the voice belonged.

Since I couldn't photograph the questioner, I'll photograph the questions, I said to myself. And so I did.

I photographed the empty hills. I photographed the burned-down village. I photographed the wolves howling on the hills in the middle of the day.

I entered a house in ruins and photographed the empty crib.

Often, in the mountain, I sit at the foot of a rock and talk to myself: When the clouds disperse, you will see the eastern summit, through your binoculars, you will see rocks shifting, when the sun is in your eyes, lower your binoculars or you'd go blind.

DREAM/FALL

At daybreak, I am sitting at the foot of a rock. A fur coat on my back. I am shivering. It's not true: Fur doesn't keep you warm. My teeth are clattering. Down below is a stream. Wolves are howling. No village in sight. Not a house, no chimney smoke. Day breaks. Slowly, slowly, everything is illuminated. That's when I see a boat on the river down below. An old man in it. Alone. Struggling to pull in his fishing nets. The boat drifting in the currents. The nets must be heavy. I focus my binoculars. The sun is brighter. The nets filled with enormous fish. Human size. I zoom in. No, not fish. Corpses.

Human corpses. I wanted to scream but couldn't. I wanted to run but couldn't. I wanted to wake up but couldn't. Eventually, I mustered a scream. The old fisherman unloosed his net and looked at me.

I leaped off the cliff and was at the river's edge.

Don't be afraid, he said. These dead are harmless.

I looked. As if, for the first time, I was the one looking, the one seeing, speaking. And not just with humans. With animals, too, with trees, with rocks.

I can write on the snow, I can sleep on the snow.

I need no one. I need only these human beings. Because they suffer like I do. I understand them. No, I can't. I can't understand them either. They stare at me absently. When I speak, they neither ask a question nor smile nor cry. They just stare at me, puzzled. Puzzled, I stare back. I want to look with their eyes. At myself, at them, at the world.

Our ancient books ask: Why would anyone leave home?
These mountains are your country.
If the wolf broke into the pen, would you abandon your flock?
The lambs, the yearlings, the rams, the sheep, all are yours.
He who tasted pain, would he beat his knees?
Tell me, would he? Would he beat his foolish head against rocks?
Wouldn't he stop and think?
Wouldn't he join hands?
Wouldn't he say, I'm wounded, you're wounded, we're wounded?
Would he say nothing, would he not speak, say nothing, nothing?

The man turned the lock in the dark.

Saw the woman waiting for him in the glow of the oil lamp.

Are you back? the woman asked.

The man did not reply.

Who are you? the woman asked.

The man said, Be quiet.

The woman let out a scream loud enough to rouse the mountain, the wolves, the dogs.

Guns rained down bullets.

The dead.

Lamps extinguished.

In the dark, no one saw the dead.

Except maybe the dogs.

What kind of snow is this, I asked.

Haven't you seen worse, Teacher? he asked. It's only spring.

Spring? I asked. Snowy spring?

Whichever, Vahap said. Snowy spring, spring winter, call it what you will.

You can't even see the sky, I said. Whatalota spring snow is this?

It'll clear out soon, Teacher, he said, gesturing toward the invisible summit. Soon it'll clear out.

Then again, at night, the wolves might come down. One never knows. Then it means darkwinter, darkbloodwinter is here.

Here time doesn't exist, my guide says. So you know.
Don't tell me that, I say. Never tell me that.
I'm telling the truth, he says.
Never ever tell the truth, I said.
Here, my stubborn guide continued, it's morning, then evening,
at night you go to bed, then you wake up, morning again. Always
the same. Never different.

The hunter gazed at the mountains, at the jagged cliffs, the
summit covered in clouds.
As if it got cold suddenly, he shivered down to his marrow.
If time doesn't exist here, what does? the hunter asked, his jaw
trembling.
The guide replied without a moment's hesitation.
Only death. Would you say death knows time?
I don't know, the hunter said.
I'll tell you, the guide said. It doesn't.

Before I take a step, I think.

I always have. Especially on the snow. One can slide and fall on the snow. Fall and die. I always think first: Where am I going? Do I have to go? What if I don't go? Will I be able to return? What will I see if I go? Who will I talk with? What will he tell me? Would he tell me how he died? (Because it's all death here.)

*I had five lambs, three yearlings. And two dogs. I herded them to the city, thinking, I'll sell them and go away from here. My five lambs, three yearlings, two dogs, and I made it to the city. I sold the lambs and the yearlings. I let the dogs loose. I got on the bus. At Hoşap River, they waylaid us. Does it matter who? They took my money and my life. I feel sorry for my dogs.*

I knew that desperate man. Told him, Let's escape together. I can't anymore, he said. You can escape only once in life. You also escaped here, didn't you? Don't go back. Stay with us. What can you do—it's life.

When I take a step, I also think of the next step.

I can't help it. When I take my first step, I already know my tenth, hundredth, thousandth step. Besides, after a few steps you're not yourself. You're not the one taking the steps. You're not the one pulling the trigger. But the eye, like it or not, sees the roads, the turns, the precipice, the summit, and it commits them to memory.

What else is life?


*Note: Strange, isn't it, to be the same human being everywhere, to live as if you're the same human being.*

And from here on you will not be and I will
And from here on we won't sit together and sip our tea
And from here on women will die even babies will
And from here on the Great Zab will flow scarlet
And from here on reason will disappear
And from here on cruelty will disappear
And from here on blood-red snow will fall
And from here on the mountains will hear no songs
And from here on only wolves will howl in the mountains
And from here on no stone upon a stone
And from here on the Great Zab will wash the corpses to
its shores those dispossessed nameless unmourned dead with
unrecognizable faces
And from here on a long freezing winter an endless winter
And from here on no more

I had a dream that night.

An old white-bearded man enters my room, a huge burlap sack on his shoulder, he empties it on the floor.

Here, he says, the supplies you asked for.

I look at the pile in the middle of the room and see words, each in the form of an object, in different shapes, of different substance, thousands of words. I arrange them like fortunes, line them up and form sentences. One after another. In this way I am making my book, not writing it. When I turn to thank the old man, I notice he is gone—or I wake up from my dream, get out of bed, perform my ablutions (God forgive me), and make tea. While the tea is steeping, I open my notebook with yellow leaves and begin to write: If one day your path takes you to these desolate mountains . . .

Does it never rain around here? he asked.

It does, I said. Depends on the season.

What do you mean, depends on the season.

Surely you've heard of the rainy season, I said. Or the season of death, the killing season, the season of fear, the season of fires, the season of migration, haven't you heard of these either?

I have, he said, but had never experienced them.

So now you have, I said.

*Bikin ku hûn nemirin.*

Try not to die.

Who needs a well around here, I said.

Water gushes out of every crack.

Blood and water, to be precise. Don't you see?

No cemeteries either.

Back in the old days, yes, but not anymore.

Take a pickax and dig.

You'll see it's graves everywhere.

You come here, you look around, but you don't see.

You want to talk with people, you don't know their language.

Talk with the dead.

You must've dreamed it, I said.

No, he said, I didn't. My eyes were open.

Then you must've dreamed with your eyes open.

No, it was freezing, I was shivering.

Smoking a cigarette to keep myself warm.

Did you roll your cigarette with your frozen fingers?

No, you gave me the cigarette. You lit it with your lighter.

I did?

Don't talk like you don't remember.

You were sitting next to me. You saw it with me.

Then what did I say?

Be quiet, you said. Don't speak. Look there, you said, gesturing with your hand.

I saw what you showed me.

And what you didn't. Or didn't see yourself.

They were digging holes in the frozen ground and burying the dead, naked, without shrouds.

Women beating their chests. Their elegies . . .

I didn't understand the words but recognized the tune.

Everyone knows the music of death, isn't that so? I said.

I left when the sun was setting. In the distance I saw wolves muzzling the bloody snow.

Here the words here the dreams here the thoughts here the
signs here the images here the symbols here the stories here
the people here the tears here the death here the animals
here the mountains here the streams here the rivers here the
lakes here the guns
here the grenades here the tanks
here the jets here the helicopters
here the cliffs here the caves
here the words the words the words


What I need now is a welding torch.
To join these together, to make them whole, all of them,
side by side, one on top of the other, shoulder to shoulder,
jaw to jaw, to lock them together into a world, to make a
world
In the name of this wrecked, grieving, fatal world

This was a long journey.
We only saw gorges and rivers along the way.
Never human beings.
Never trees.
Only dogs.
And at night only jackals.

(SUMMARY)

They love singing.
Shooting guns.
Rice pilaf with plenty of butter.
Weaving kilims.
Giving birth.
Herbed cheese.
The spring sun.
Looking at the stars.
Riding horses.
Men and women, lining their eyes with kohl.
Of trees, the poplar.
Of animals, the rabbit.
They live with dogs, they don't like dogs.
They like making fire in the mountains.
—Especially at night—
They say little. They like silence.
Watching the snow fall, its sound and color.


As if they worship the mountain, the sun and fire—
They have an odd sense of weekdays.
On Sunday, if you say it's Monday,
they believe you.
If you say Friday, they don't.
They don't know Saturday at all.
They know how to add and subtract

but not to multiply or divide.
They don't use pencil or paper.
They commit everything to memory.
Gather and recall.
They lie all the time.
They love children.
—It's unclear if they love these mountains or not—


As if they never think: What would the mountains do if we
left.
But they don't speak what they think.
The wolves are their enemy.
But not only the wolves.
Humans too.
They kill the wolves and the humans.
They believe in God and maybe in nothing else.
They seldom use money.
Because they have no money. They barter and exchange.
They wake at sunrise.
They tend sheep—just the children—
They chop wood—just the men—
They roll out dough—just the women—
They go to bed soon after sunset.
They have Ağas, none of them wealthy.
They take multiple wives. Therefore they have many children.
Too many children die too soon.
"God gives, God takes away," they say,
digging a hole in the snow and burying them.
Like their births, their deaths are not recorded.
As if the dead had never been born.
In the evening before sleep, they thank God for what they
have.

They all have good eyesight.
Even those who can't see well don't use glasses—maybe because they've seen everything already and nothing new enters their field of vision.
Women have long hair, without henna, full of lice.
Their eyes round and black and kohled.

*Mountains, rivers, humans, deaths, majnuns, hunters, villagers . . .*
*They wore me out, the Man says.*
*You mean words, the Woman says.*
*And words, the Man says. You have a point. Inevitably.*
*But wasn't* this *always the point, the Woman says.*
*No. Not* this. *Not always.*
*Didn't you travel for* this, *the Woman says.*
*No. This, too. Maybe. Possibly.*
*But the goal wasn't* this.
*What was it, then, the Woman says.*
*The journey itself, the Man says.*
*I see. And now that it's ended?*
*What's ended? the Man says.*
*The journey, the Woman says.*
*The real journey is just starting, the Man says.*
*Back on that unbearable road again? the Woman says.*
*Whether I want to or not, the Man says.*
*Stop trying in vain, the Woman says. You'll never be able to write what you've seen, heard, and lived there.*
*Then I'd write what I dreamed, the Man says.*
*As always, the Woman says.*
*As always, the Man says.*
*Then don't wait, the Woman says. Write. Here is the paper. Here is the pencil.*

# EASTERN TALES

First time I set foot there
—years ago, many years ago—
I assumed I'd understand these people.
I'd come from far away; we didn't speak each other's languages.
Though, truth be told, I didn't worry much about that.
Common language, I knew, didn't mean common words.
In that mountain village,
for a long, white winter,
I lived among them.
Our everyday troubles we understood well enough.
Our needs turned out to be (nearly) the same.
But not our loneliness.
I'd say they had no problem called loneliness.
Or they were not aware of it.
Or theirs was an altogether different loneliness I couldn't
recognize.
I don't know.
What I know is this: The closer I got to them
the more distant they became.
The closer they got to me
the more distant I became.


"Teacher, what's the news on the radio?"
I'd summarize it for them.
But the news wasn't their news.
It didn't concern them.

They killed as much as they died.
Asking them why
was like banging my head against rocks.
"Why do you kill each other?"
No one seemed to understand my question.

An entire winter passed like this.
I taught their children reading, writing, counting, addition,
subtraction, multiplication, division. A bit of
life sciences and civics.
Yes, I managed that much.

Then I gave my radio to the village mayor.
My boots, my galoshes, my woolen undershirt,
my socks, I handed out to the villagers.
I stuffed my books and notebooks in a bag,
and when the snow started to melt, I left the village.

Years later, as I leaf through the notebooks,
I see that these people and I,
who didn't speak each other's languages,
had understood one another.
I don't know what language we had in common,
nor do I want to know.
Our common language didn't change them
but it changed me. I'm sure of it.
Every passing day returns to me the traces
of our shared life in that mountain village;
I see them. I live them.
And these words I've been scrawling through the years
are those traces, words wounded like me.

# MİRZA

THE VILLAGE mayor had already taken his fourth wife and had seven children with her (Mansur, Yakup, Hajer, Kasım, Gülhan, Şerif, Mukaddes). In total, the Mayor had twenty-seven children, that is, if we don't count the ones who died, which he didn't.

Four of his children (Yakup, Murad, Bedirhan, Abbas) were married, that is, if we don't count the daughters, which he didn't. His sons had twelve children from their first marriages. Yakup had two, Murad four, Bedirhan three, and Abbas three. Three of Murad's children, two of Bedirhan's, and one of Abbas's had died. None of Yakup's children died. Though who knows why, he had stopped at two. His wife had not delivered any for the last three years. Which made Yakup start thinking of a second marriage at age twenty-four.

The Mayor started thinking that he was an old man, that he would soon leave this world. These mud-brick houses stacked against one another were like a maze, and at times he would lose his way walking from one to the next. In his dreams, he saw an immense house, like a palace. Built of stone. Two levels. Maybe even three. Why not?

Yet there was no mason around these parts who could build his dream house. The architects and stone masons who built those large buildings in the city had come from other cities and left once they completed the job. The Mayor had heard about the beauty of the Mardin houses, about the Mardin stonemasons, their fine skills and knowledge. One day he couldn't resist and described his dream to Yakup, his eldest son, and asked him to bring a master mason from Mardin. Yakup had never been to Mardin. But he was his father's favorite, plus he needed his father's help to take another wife.

An immense house. Like a palace. Made of stone too.
Yakup also lost himself in this dream.
A kitchen with five stoves. An oven so big that it could bake bread for the whole village. The rooms bright and warm . . .
Yakup went to Mardin. He saw that the city was full of stone houses like the ones that filled his father's (and little by little his own) dreams.

The locals sipping tea at the inn where he was staying asked him what he'd come looking for, and he told them that he needed a stonemason. They gave him at least ten names.
The next day, Yakup found these master masons.
(Mardin was bigger than his village but still small enough that everyone knew one another.)
Some listened smiling. Some asked how much Yakup would pay. (The matter of payment had not occurred to him, nor had his father mentioned anything about it.)
Only one of them (Mirza, as he was called) said, "I heard a lot about your parts but never visited, might as well go and see first."
They set out together.

Once in the village, Mirza showed no sign of surprise.
The Mayor, not quite sold on this scrubby Mardin man,

decided he'd host him overnight and, after dinner, described his dream house to Master Mirza.

The more he described, the more his enthusiasm grew. The Mardin man listened quietly.

"What do you think?" asked the Mayor. "Can you build me a house like this?"

"I'm a stonemason," Mirza replied, his voice almost a whisper.

Did he mean he could or couldn't?

No, he could build it. "But is there a stone pit around these parts?" he asked.

The Mayor looked confused. This was the first time he was hearing "stone" and "pit" uttered side by side.

"We have stones and we have pits," he said. "But what is a stone pit?"

Couldn't he see—the mountains were covered with stones. The Mardin man smiled. "You can't build the house you want with those stones."

The Mayor was still confused.

"To build the house walls, you need special stones excavated from stone pits. These stones here are good for garden walls." (The Mayor hadn't heard this one either.) "But if you built the house walls with them, they'd collapse."

The Mayor felt as if he'd fallen off a horse.

Where did Yakup find such a strange fellow!

He couldn't even speak their language well; the Mayor wasn't sure he understood most of what he was saying.

Caught in the Mayor's exasperated stare, the Mardin man said, "You could use mud bricks and build a big, multistory house, but not with the soil you have around here."

"And what's wrong with the soil?"

The Mardin man smiled. "That, I'll tell you tomorrow."

He took out his silver tobacco case and rolled a cigarette, handing it to the Mayor, then he rolled one for himself.

They lit their cigarettes and smoked in silence, just eyeing each other.

That night, the Mayor, his son Yakub, and the Mardin man slept in the same room.

When they woke at dawn, their guest had been out, taking a walk around the village. The Mayor performed his ablutions, while Mirza inspected the walls of the houses. He scoped the mountain slopes. At the village fountain, he rinsed his mouth and drank a couple of palmfuls.

Back in the house, he noticed that the Mayor had waited for him to sit for the morning prayer.

"I already prayed," he said.

That day, he described to the Mayor and his son how to mix the mud bricks for a large house, how many arm spans the foundation needed to be, how thick the walls . . .

"I can't keep all this in my head," the Mayor said, and called for the Teacher, asking him to write down everything that the Mardin man specified.

The Teacher wrote everything down. The dimensions of the windows. The height of the ceiling. The floor beams. The type of lumber to use. Once he was done with all the specifications, Mirza took the pencil from the Teacher and sketched a plan. Then he called the Mayor outside. Pointing at the southern slope, he said, "If you're going to build your house, build it there. If you follow my instructions, your house will outlast you, even if it's made of mud bricks."

"It will?" the Mayor asked. "A big mud-brick house, even a very big one, even two or three stories high, would outlast me?"

"You can build a château with the right kind of mud bricks, if you want."

Château?

The Mayor had not heard this word either.

At lunch, they ate rabbit stew—the rabbit shot just this morning—pilaf, and yogurt. Then they drank tea.

His work done, the Mardin man was ready to leave.

The Mayor felt that he had to pay him for his work (not that he had done much—besides coming here from Mardin, staying three days, giving some instructions, drawing a sketch, showing where to set the house, and so on). But the Mayor didn't have money, and he wasn't keen on parting with one of the fourteen gold coins he kept in his sash to pay this man called Mirza, a mason from Mardin.

"For your troubles, would you settle for a ewe and three yearlings?" he asked.

"It was no trouble," the Mardin man replied. "A ewe and three yearlings—that's too much. It'd be a hassle to take them all the way to Mardin. The ewe should be enough."

The Mayor picked the skinniest ewe in his pen, but he made sure the women prepared a food sack for him.

As he was about to leave, the Mardin man said, "I'd heard of a roundaround somewhere nearby. Might as well see it while I'm here."

The Mayor was hearing this word for the first time, too.

Mirza described what a roundaround was: A labyrinth, a structure made of stone walls and pathways built to confound the visitor who gets lost and sometimes can't find his way out.

The Mayor and the villagers understood what he was looking for.

"Yes," they confirmed, in the meadow between the two abandoned Assyrian villages, those round walls from ancient times, fallen in places but mostly standing, with doors no one dares to enter through, no roof, empty, built who knows why, though some say to house the insane who lived on the food scraps tossed over the walls, who lived and died there, though others say it was to house ancient gods where humans would never be able to find them, except when the gods themselves wished to come out and show their faces to humans. Yet another legend spoke of an outlaw who lived in the time of the padishahs, or maybe earlier, who had built the place as his hideaway since no one would venture in, and if they did, they'd be trapped and fall prey to the outlaw.

The Mardin man listened with a gentle smile across his lips. But if it had no roof, how did the crazies or the gods or the outlaw survive the accursed winters?

A villager responded, "It had to have a roof then; must've collapsed since."

"I see," the Mardin man said and left it there.

Then he asked, "Is it too far from here?"

Yes, certainly by foot.

What about on horseback?

One could go anywhere on horseback.

Even to Mount Kaf.

But why did he want to go?

"Curiosity," the Mardin man replied.

The Mayor looked at his son, as if to say, "In all of Mardin, you couldn't find someone other than this crazy fellow?"

And Yakup looked back at his father, as if to say, "No one else wanted to come!"

The Mardin man asked the Mayor if his son might take him there.

The Mayor stammered.

"What's there to see. Not a soul nor a jinn. Nobody has set foot there since the Assyrians emptied their villages and left."

"Then mine can be the first foot."

"My son can get you there all right, but how will you get back?"

"I'll find a way. How long would it take?"

"Three or four hours on horseback."

"Then let's go," the Mardin man said.

"And what will you do with the ewe?"

"I'll take her with me."

"Then you won't get there before sundown," said the Mayor.

"I'll carry her on my lap; I've nothing else with me."

They saddled two horses.

Yakup mounted one, and Mirza the other.

Mirza set the ewe in front of him—three of her legs had been tied together with twine—and the food sack in the back. Then they rode away.

The Mayor and all the villagers watched in puzzlement.

In the afternoon, they stopped to rest in the first Assyrian village that had been abandoned years ago.

Yakup dismounted. The Mardin man handed the ewe to Yakup. Then, getting off his horse, he took the ewe back, untied her legs and set her loose.

Then he started looking at the houses, one by one, rubbing the wall ruins with his hand.

"See?" he told Yakup. "These houses were made of stone. Once upon a time there must've been a stone pit nearby, and stonemasons."

He entered one of the houses. Looked right, then left, as if searching for something. When he exited the ruins, the vague expression on his face divulged nothing about whether he'd found what he was searching for.

"Where was the fountain?" he asked Yakub.

"I wouldn't know," Yakup replied, perplexed. "This is my first time in the village."

"There was supposed to be a fountain," Mirza said, "north side of the village."

They walked north, away from the houses, and reached a small stone-tiled area (although now wild grass sprang up among the cracks). The fountain stood there. Dry rubble. Only its stone basin had survived.

"Fine, then," Mirza said. "We saw this village too. Let's go." He walked to the ewe that was grazing. Using the same twine, he tied together her back legs and her left front leg before handing her to Yakup. He mounted his horse, took the ewe from Yakup and set her on his lap. He rode without looking back.

Reaching the top of the hill, they could see the roundaround in the distance. And on the southern slope opposite them stood another abandoned village that resembled the one they had stopped in earlier.

"We won't get to see that one," said Mirza.

He looked at the roundaround down at the foot of the valley. To get there, they'd have to descend the sharp slope covered with rocks and thornbush.

Yakup got scared, "Going down is easy, but how do I climb back up? How do I get back to the village before sundown?"

The Mardin man, without taking his eyes away from the roundaround in the distance, said, "From here on, it's my path. Please hold the ewe one more time."

Yakup (thoroughly relieved) got off his horse and took the ewe.

The Mardin man, too, got off his horse. He untied the ewe's legs. Tied a rope around her neck.

"You go back now," he told Yakup. "Will you make it before sundown?"

"I will," Yakup replied. "If I can't, I'll spend the night in Gezne. What are you going to do here?"

The Mardin man tossed his food sack over his shoulder and, extending his hand to Yakup, said, "Forgive my wrongs, son."

"And you mine," Yakup replied.

Yakup's eyes and his heart burned with the dread of a human being facing the unknown.

"And what are you going to do?"

A vague smile in his eyes, Mirza repeated, "I'll go see it."

"Will you go inside?"

"That's why I came here."

"What if you can't get out?"

"I'll try."

Try. Yakup heard the word as if it wasn't a word in his language. And maybe it wasn't.

"Fare you well," Yakup said.

"You, too, son."

Yakup now felt in his heart a different feeling, one he couldn't name, something akin to pity, to pleading.

"If you want . . ." he said. "If you want . . . I'll wait while you go down . . . we can return together afterward."

The Mardin man, turning his gaze away from the round-around, looked at Yakup.

"Don't worry about me. Go back to your village."

Then he walked toward the incline, the ewe by his side, the food sack on his shoulder.

Yakup walked for a while with a heavy stride. He thought of turning around and looking. He did. The Mardin man and the ewe had disappeared among the rocks and the thornbush. Yakup rode his horse, leading the other horse behind him. He had learned from this man things he had not known to this day. But what had he learned? How to make the mud bricks strong, how far apart to set the beams, the depth of the foundation or the consistency of the mortar—surely this wasn't all he had learned. Back in the village, when Mirza was giving his instructions and the Teacher was writing them down, Yakup had listened carefully and learned these things. But now, on his way back, he sensed that he had learned other things, things more important, but what they were (besides mud bricks, beams, foundation, what have you), he couldn't name.

Mirza took a breather. Looked at the roundaround again. This maze that no one dared enter had appeared long ago in a small child's dreams. Everyone would tell stories about the roundaround, and the child would believe everything he heard. But to truly believe them, he had to go inside the roundaround. He was scared. What if he couldn't find his way out, as in the stories?
Mirza tugged at the ewe's rope.
"Let's go. Let's get there before sundown," he said.
Once again skipping and darting like a gazelle among the rocks and the thornbush, he descended to the valley.

He could feel his heart pulsing in his mouth. One day in May when the snows ended and the grass began to turn green, the child had picked a ewe and a lamb from his flock and, without telling anyone, taken to the road. Feeding the lamb with the ewe's milk on the way, he had crossed this same hill and reached this downward path.

Gazing at the roundaround in the distance, he descended the slope with such elation that, even before he was halfway down, his entire body was covered with scrapes and cuts from the rocks and the thornbush. His shirt—already mended in a thousand places—was ripped to shreds, and his scrapes and cuts were bleeding. Just then he heard the familiar barking of his dog, who had left the flock behind to follow the young shepherd and, tumbling down the hill, was drawing near to him. The sight of his dog filled his heart with confidence, making him forget the sting of his bleeding wounds.

Reaching the valley, the Mardin man felt no fatigue. Instinctively, he turned to look behind him. There was only the ewe. "Stop," he said, as if the animal would understand. "There used to be a stream around here." And sure enough, he found the stream. He splashed his hands and face with the water. After rinsing his mouth twice, he drank the water and let the ewe drink. Then he sat down. Opened his food sack. But he wasn't hungry. He wasn't hungry at all.

He was staring at the roundaround that stood maybe a hundred steps ahead. "Ruins," he said. Walking closer, his ewe, her lamb, and his dog following, the first thing he did was to look for the stream. All four of them heartily quenched their thirst.

He cut two sturdy branches and sharpened their ends with his knife. He stuck one of the stakes in the ground by the east gate of the roundaround and the other by the west gate. He then tied his dog to the pole by the east gate, and the ewe to the other by the west gate. Then he examined the walls of the roundaround. They didn't seem man-made. Built as they were with stones too large for any human being to carry, much less stack on top of each other.
He circled the roundaround twice, rubbing his hand against the stones; then, prying the lamb away from her mother, he walked to the east gate. Although scared, he was determined to enter. To see with his own eyes whether the stories he'd heard were true or not.

The dog kept barking, as if begging the boy not to enter. But since he had come this far, he would have to enter.

And that's what he did in the end. After walking a stretch, he noticed that the inside walls were thinner. The round-around had no lookouts or roof. He could see the sky. The anxious lamb, darting left, right, forward, and back, guided them through the narrow paths between the walls. At times, the boy had the distinct feeling that they were walking the same path over. But there were no markers, no signs of human visitors along the paths. No skull, no bones, as if someone had walked through and cleaned the place the day before. After a while, the lamb's bleating sounded different. Either the animal had overcome his panic, or he sensed that they were nearing the exit.

The boy didn't hear the dog's barking either. But he was no longer scared. Now right now left then right again, they kept moving forward just the same. Except that they had stopped walking the same paths over. The journey continued until a new light—not from the sky above but from the land ahead—illuminated their path.

How long had they been walking?

He didn't know.

The boy and the lamb walked toward that light.

Near the exit, he heard the bleating of the ewe. The lamb, with unexpected agility, bolted toward the gate.

"Anyone could have succeeded," said the Mardin man, as if talking to someone standing in front of him.

It had to take these many years to prove that he hadn't dreamed it.

He got up, walked toward the east gate.

# THE STORY OF IBRAM, SON OF IBRAM

I HEARD their story from Halit.

Between late April and early May, when the snows turned to slush, the sunny days began to return, and the bears started leaving their caves at the end of a long winter sleep, I was out one morning with Halit, who had been trying to interest me in hunting, and we decided to stop and catch our breath, after slogging through the wet snow.

As I sat in the hollow of a rock, lit the cigarette Halit had rolled for me, and stared into the distance where two hills closing on each other formed a mountain pass, I saw a hamlet made of three or four houses shrouded in the morning fog.

Chilled to my bones and craving a hot cup of tea, I told Halit, "Let's go take a look," but he refused. "We're out hunting, Teacher, not strolling." Failing to see the point of his objection, I tried to insist, but to no avail: "No, no, not *there*."

In this region where it was considered the custom to stop by every house in every village along the way and enjoy a cup of tea, I didn't understand Halit's reaction. Reading perhaps the confusion in my eyes, he said, "We can't visit that village when I'm with you," adding in vague, half-veiled words that I shouldn't go on my own either.

As he spoke, he looked away, not at me or at the cluster of houses and the trees that came into clearer view as the morning fog subsided. Restless, he turned his back first to me, then to the cliffs, then to the village below, staring straight at the mountain summit. "No," he said, "I can't do it. It'd be unbecoming of me to go with you."

I understood nothing. Remained silent.

"We came to hunt, let's go hunt."

I repeated what I had already told him a thousand times: "I don't enjoy hunting. I enjoy drinking tea with people I don't know."

"Go then," Halit said, his back still facing me.

What's the harm in going down and stopping by a house to drink their tea?

"To each his own hunt," I said, standing up. I handed my rifle to Halit. "Take this, if you don't mind. I'll meet you back in the village."

As if he heard none of my words, Halit turned around and this time looked me in the eye.

"That's Ibram's village," he said. "Trust me, I can't go there. I can't, even if I wanted to." Then, as if talking not to me but to the mountain or the prey he was dreaming of hunting, he added, "Don't insist. And don't go, either."

"Which Ibram? Who is this Ibram?" I asked.

"My cellmate in the penitentiary, didn't I tell you already?"

"Why, then, you can say hi to his mother, father, his wife or children."

"I can't. He has no father, mother, wife, or children."

"Then what's the risk?" I said, trying to smile.

"You're right. No risk. Still, if you're my friend, you shouldn't go down either. Let's mind our business. If you insist, I'll tell you Ibram's story one day so you know why I don't want to go down there myself."

I didn't insist.

Instead of descending to the valley stretched out below us, we headed north toward the hills.

We followed the tracks of a female bear and her cub in the snow. Thankfully, we shot nothing.

Before sundown, when we returned to the village empty-handed and tired, I didn't ask Halit about Ibram. Neither did he say anything.
Only: "You chase away the prey, Teacher," he said. "I'll never go hunting with you again."
He was smiling.
Mimicking his awkward smile, I said, "Then what's to eat tonight?"
"The usual. Bread and herbed cheese," he said. "But if you like, I'll slaughter the last lamb for you."
"I'm not that hungry," I said. We parted.

One evening, several days later, we were drinking our tea by the tin stove, listening to world news and weather among the crackle on the radio, when Halit resumed our conversation, as if no time had lapsed and we were still sitting in the hollow of that rock, puffing on the cigarettes he had rolled for us.
"Teacher, how uncurious you are," he said, "you listen to the world's news in all those languages—some I understand, some I don't—but you're not curious enough to ask about the people around you."
"You're right, Halit. The city folk are like that."
"I'm never going out hunting with you."
"You already told me that," I said, searching for a radio station in a language I understood.
"Because you love people and bears just the same . . ." he said.
The radio was broadcasting the day's news.
"You're wrong," I said.
"Yet you're never curious about them."
"Who?"
"People. Human beings."

Which ones? The ones in the city, those in the village? Or the ones mentioned in the news? I was going to ask but didn't.

"I'll have another tea," he said.

I took the kettle from the stove and filled his cup.

"What's the radio saying?"

"Not much. Some people again screwing some other people."

"Just like here."

"More or less."

We sipped our tea.

"So, aren't you going to tell me?"

"What?"

"What you've been wanting to tell me."

"Ibram's story?"

"Was that his name?"

"Yes, both his and his father's."

"Strange."

"The names aren't what's strange."

"What is then?"

"What life dealt Ibram."

"Which Ibram?"

"Ibram the son."

"Care for some more tea?"

"Not yet."

Me, filling my cup: "So what happened to Ibram that we couldn't visit his house and accept a cup of his tea?"

"Long story."

"Then we'll sit here tonight, drink our tea, and you'll tell me this long story of Ibram."

"There's no such thing as Ibram's story."

Me, growing impatient: "So what's there?"

Halit, sipping his tea, lost in thought: "There is my cellmate, Ibram. And there is his father, Ibram."

Me, tired of the news, searching for a different station: "Then we'll hear the stories of two Ibrams at once."

Halit, finished with his tea: "Actually their stories are one and the same."

"Got it. And why didn't we go down to their village?"

"I'll tell you that later."

"What'll you tell me now?"

"Ibram's story."

"Will you roll me a cigarette?"

"May that be all you need."

Me, while Halit rolls the cigarette: "So two Ibrams share one story."

Halit, handing me the cigarette: "Yes. Just as you said."

"What?"

"I don't know."

"So go on, tell whatever it is that you will."

Halit, rolling a cigarette for himself: "Where to start? Sometimes I think you do want to know us, and maybe more than we want to know ourselves. Other times, it's like you haven't been here, like you don't know us at all. The conversations, what people tell you, like you don't listen."

"That's all right. Go ahead and tell it still."

Halit remained silent.

He finished his tea and turned the cup upside down.

"You're not listening to me, Teacher."

It was true. I wasn't listening to him. Or to myself.

Or the radio. As though I was somewhere else, someone else. As though the man facing me was a stranger who spoke in a strange language.

"Forgive me," was all I could say. "You're right. You should tell me Ibram's story some other evening."

"But I have to tell it now, right away," said Halit. "That's why I came here. Besides, I don't have too much time."

"Not tonight," I said. "Tonight, I don't have the mind to listen to anyone's story. I want to die."

"What did you say, Teacher?" Startled, Halit rose to his feet. "What a thing to say! Never let the thought visit you again!"

"I want to sleep," I said.

"Thought I heard something else," he said, standing by the door, about to leave.

"Good night, Halit," I said.

"Good night, Teacher. You all right? Nothing's wrong with you, is it?"

"Yes, I'm fine. But tonight, I won't be able to listen to Ibram's story or to anything."

"So be it," Halit said. "Maybe tomorrow evening."

"I don't know. Maybe."

"Sleep well."

"You too."

As he was leaving, he said, "You know I don't sleep at night."

I didn't sleep either and, as soon as Halit left, I started writing the story that had begun taking shape in my mind while he was talking.

THE SUMMIT

*I asked one of the villagers: Is it possible to reach the summit? In return, he asked three questions: Reach the summit? In this season? What for?*

*Nothing in particular. I'm just asking, is it possible to reach the summit?*

*Of course, he said. If you're strong enough and you know why you want to.*

*I didn't know why except that whenever I looked up there, I wanted to be there. Maybe in order to see from the summit the other side of the mountain. This desire, I am sure, derived from a certain sense of powerlessness, rather than of strength. In the end, I also was a human being. I also wanted to strive, to reach somewhere. To go beyond. To see what I hadn't yet seen. To make it there, and to return.*

*(Where did you go?*
*To the summit.*
*What did you accomplish?*
*An ascent of the summit.*
*What did you see?*
*All the mountains. All the prairies.)*

*One morning, we finished our tea, ate our herbed cheese wrapped inside our* yufka *bread, and started out.*
*Luckily for us, there was no blizzard, no snow.*
*Before reaching the summit, I thought my heart would stop.*
*It always happens, the villager climbing with me said. It's the altitude.*
*But once at the summit, I felt not a trace of fatigue.*
*That's what happens at the summit, said the villager, my companion.*
*Are there times when one doesn't reach the summit?*
*Plenty.*
*Fear of the wolves?*
*Not only wolves. Sometimes the heart gives up. It just cracks.*
*And then?*
*Then we leave him in the snow. In the spring, once the ice melts, we go find the corpse. Frozen. We perform the rites and bury him where he died.*
*No one comes asking or looking for them?*
*Around here, no one looks for anyone. Even if they did, they won't find anyone. And if they come looking for him? He died and was buried here, we tell them. People don't ask many questions.*

*I took a deep breath.*

*Let's go down the other side of the mountain, I said.*

*What for? he asked. That side's the same as this side. The same houses there as here, the same villages, the same human beings, the same poverty, the same death. Let's go back the way we came.*

*As we began descending, I heard gunshots.*

*My companion: Let's keep to our path. It's either the gendarmes or others. Hunting wolves or humans.*


Moments ago, I took a pinch of shag-cut, golden-yellow Bitlis tobacco from the case Halit handed me, and I rolled a cigarette as if I'd always rolled my cigarettes. Halit's eyes were on me. Attentively, he watched my hands, the way my fingers rolled the paper, as if he were trying to commit my movements to memory. When I gave him back the tobacco case, our eyes met.

"You can tell me Ibram's story tonight," I said.

I lit my cigarette. Exhaling the smoke through my nose, I craned my neck back and watched the shadow play on the ceiling created by the trembling flame of the kerosene lamp.

"What a strange fellow you are, Teacher. Now, right now, you're a person I'll never understand."

I didn't respond.

No doubt, I was.

"I swear you have moments like nothing exists in the world. Even you don't exist. How do you do that? Were you like this before you arrived here, or did it happen since you mixed in with us? Is it the mountain air, this snow, this curse of a winter, the silence, the poverty, the despair that made you like this?"

I got up from the straw mat, took the teakettle off the stove, and poured a cup for Halit and one for myself. Handing him his tea, I asked, "Did you say something?"

"No, nothing," Halit replied.

"Then someone else must have."

"Possibly. Though I didn't hear a word."

We laughed.

I walked to the window. Outside was pitch-black. No light or stars.

"Will you tell me Ibram's story tonight? Look, it's dark outside. Not a soul nor a jinn around. Even the dogs aren't howling. If you want to tell it, it's the perfect time."

"I can't decide where to start."

"It doesn't matter, as long as you start. That's the tough part; the rest follows anyhow."

"No, I'll start all right but I don't think the end will come. Ibram's story isn't finished yet."

"Then start at the end."

"I can't do things backward like you," Halit said. "I'm not smart enough."

"Who is Ibram? Who is the other Ibram? Who is the son, who is the father? Is there a mother, are there other children? Why is Ibram in prison? Who did he kill and why? Start out with these."

"How you change so suddenly, Teacher, I don't understand you. You just rolled a fine cigarette with your slender fingers, like you've been rolling cigarettes for a thousand years, then you got lost in the smoke, finished your tea, then your cigarette, like I wasn't here nor were you; but now you cram the room with all these people. Like you already know the story I'm about to tell. And maybe how it ends, too. How do I tell a story to someone like you?"

"I'm listening, Halit."

"Then turn off that radio."

I did and was startled by the silence. As if silence had a mass that filled the room. I sensed it not in my ears but in the air I breathed. All over my skin. My ears started ringing, my temples throbbing, my head spinning.

"Come on, tell the story!" I shouted.

"Ibram," Halit started in a husky voice. "You know him, Teacher, I mentioned him before. He was my cellmate."

I just nodded.

"But you don't know why he went to prison."

"Didn't he kill someone?"

"Yes."

"What kind of people are you? Can't live without killing each other?"

He smiled.

"Is that why you keep your distance at times? Why you don't ask us any questions or answer ours or tell us about the ways of the world?"

"I don't know."

"Neither do I," he said, "just like you . . . Standing here, you can up and disappear inside this room, whereas I, since I can't do what you do, I go away. To the mountains. There, I talk to myself. Hunting is the excuse, sometimes I shoot without even aiming my rifle."

"But you still hit," I said.

"Blind luck," he said, "like Ibram's."

"Then tell me about his blind luck."

The air in the room was suffocating. As if a third person, or several of them, their invisible presence, had filled the room. Maybe Halit, too, could feel this third person, these people, breathing down his neck. He sighed, then, as if divulging a secret he was supposed to keep, he said, "I'm also part of the story."

"How so? Did you kill together?"

"No," he said. "No, not yet."

My thoughts were getting scrambled. But I wanted to be here

tonight, with him, and listen to the story that he just couldn't figure out how to tell. Even before he started, I was anticipating the time when he'd leave and I'd sit at my desk to write it. Otherwise, the room's air would've suffocated me. "Look," I told Halit, "just tell me as much of the story as you want tonight. Tell me some, all, or nothing. To be honest, I'm not that curious about Ibram's story in particular. But if you want to tell it because you want to ask me something afterward, if you want my advice, just tell it and be done with it. Or else I'll go down there tomorrow, visit Ibram's house, drink his tea, and learn everything there is to learn from him."

"You'd learn nothing," Halit said, "not one thing. Because the Ibrams don't live there anymore."

"Whoever lives there would tell me."

"But that's not the same thing."

"Fine. Don't tell it, then."

"Let me ask you something first," Halit said. "If you make a promise to yourself and never whisper it to anyone's ear, do you have to keep it, no matter what?"

I understood nothing. Still, I went ahead and said, "Especially then."

"Then I have to tell it," he said. "Since I already told you this far but not the heart of it and since you answered my question to reassure me, I have to tell you Ibram's story."

He paused briefly, got off the wooden chair, and, maybe out of a former inmate's habit, began pacing from one wall to the other. Then, as if starting in the middle—although he sounded more like he was giving away the end—he said, "Ibram's father was also called Ibram."

He stopped, took a deep breath.

"Ibram went to prison for killing someone because of that grizzly father of his."

He sat on the edge of the wooden chair, tense, as if some

invisible person in the room would come and ask him to stand up. "Turn your face toward me, Teacher," he said.

His voice had suddenly changed, deepened. It sounded like someone else speaking.

I turned away from the window toward where he sat.

His eyes were bloodred, his tongue was dry, his lips were trembling, but he couldn't speak.

"What's wrong," I asked, "why did you stop?"

"Nothing yet," he stuttered, "but you should know that what I'm about to tell you tonight, no one else knows. And no one else will."

"As you wish," I said, "since no one else knows what happened and your friend Ibram is in prison."

"Everybody knows about Ibram's murder. But no one knows the truth. Now I'm going to tell it to you."

He started, at first haltingly, then self-consciously, as if addressing not just me but the entire village, the neighboring villages, and the mountains:

"One of the two neighboring houses that you saw in that hamlet belonged to the Ibrams. The other to Abdülhay. The two plots, maybe you didn't notice from a distance, are adjacent, there is no plot in between. By plot I mean a grazing field not worth plowing or sowing. Add the two and you would barely have a tenth of an acre. Let's say you have a quarter of an acre. It wouldn't even feed ten sheep. But around here you have obstinacy. Enmity. Everyone's everyone's enemy. Land feuds are not about bread money, they are about spite, about malice. One day, Ibram's father, Ibram, released his sheep and his lambs on Abdülhay's pasture. Or maybe the sheep and the lambs just jumped over the stone wall. Seeing this, Abdülhay's son Memo asked him to call his flock back. When Ibram's father, Ibram, ignored him, Memo pulled out his rifle, and when he pulled out his rifle, the other sent his dogs after him. Memo first wiped out the dogs then aimed his rifle at the old man. Ibram's father, Ibram, just stood there, on the other side of the wall, staring him down. Enraged, Memo rode his horse over the wall, grabbed the old man by his beard, and started dragging him. Ibram must have known that his son was around somewhere, so he yelled, 'Iboo!' Sure enough his son was nearby. And already on his horse. Right away he rode in the direction of his father's voice. When he reached that same rock where you and I stood the other day, his sharp eyes could see what was happening below. But he couldn't believe his eyes. So he grabbed his binoculars and, seeing that it was Memo dragging his father across the field, he charged his horse toward the valley. Memo had not noticed him riding down, probably neither had Ibram's father. Closer now, Ibram stopped again to see what was what. Memo had dragged the old man across his plot and left him among the wayward sheep. Memo had his rifle aimed at the old Ibram, but he suddenly jerked back and fell on the ground, shot by two bullets, one at his temple, the other at his neck. His blood pooled around his body. The sheep scattered about like freckled hens. When Ibram got to the pasture, his father spat at Memo's upturned body still bleeding on the ground. Ibram asked his father, 'Why did you do this?' 'The sheep,' his father replied, 'they jumped the wall.'

"'I said nothing,' Ibram told me, 'just rode my horse. Far away. I wandered in the mountains for three days, then returned to the city and turned myself in.'

"What else could he have done?"

"Is this the story of Ibram's that you couldn't tell me for days?" I asked, disappointed.

"No," Halit said, "Ibram's story started a few months after he was tried and sentenced to fifteen years."

This time I didn't ask why or how.

"At first his wife or his father would visit him once a week, or every other week. (I hadn't started my sentence yet.) Soon neither one nor the other visited anymore.

"One day (I was in the prison now) they called Ibram, he had a visitor. Seeing Abdülhay in front of him, Ibram started shaking. 'Like my blood froze suddenly,' he said. But he didn't look at him. Couldn't even utter a word. 'What could I have said?' His head lowered, staring at the floor, he just stood there. 'I waited for him to speak.' For a while, a long while, the old man didn't speak either. Then he began mumbling the words he must have been chewing in his mouth.

"'Iboo,' the old man Abdülhay started, 'you killed my son, my Memo, for the honor of your father. Now your wife and Memo's wife are widows, all the children fatherless. I'll take care of Memo's wife and children. And your father can care for your wife and children. But you should know that your father has taken your wife as his woman and made a child with her.'

"'If they slit my throat just then, I wouldn't have bled.' Ibram said. 'I raised my head and looked straight into the old man Abdülhay's eyes, but not a word escaped my parched throat.'

"Maybe old Abdülhay had come for his revenge. You don't always need a gun to take revenge. He had told the incarcerated man such things that turned the prison cell into a pit of hell.

"'Not done yet,' Abdülhay the old swine told Ibram who was staring at him like he was about to kill him, although he couldn't have done anything of this sort even if he wanted to. 'We're not neighbors anymore. Your father honored my boundary line and sold me both the house and the field.'

"'This is a game, some type of revenge,' Ibram had thought, then got up and walked back to his cell.

"When he returned, his face was as white as death. For three days, he didn't speak. Didn't eat or drink. Didn't answer any of our questions. At the end of the third day, he asked for a cup of tea, then, calmly, began to recount what Abdülhay had told him."

"So was it true?" I asked. I had goose bumps, my throat was parched.

"That's what I asked, too, Teacher, when he first told me these things. Can't be true, I told him, he came for revenge, told you all this to poison your mind, I said. But Ibram didn't doubt old Abdülhay in the least, as if he knew his father and his wife all too well. He believed everything was entirely true."

I couldn't help asking again, "But was it really true?"

"One of the fellows who was released went and saw it with his own eyes," Halit said. "Ibram's family no longer lived in their house. Neither his wife, nor his children, nor his father. Now Memo's wife and children lived in that house.

"The news didn't destroy Ibram. He was plenty destroyed already. Only, he couldn't understand why his father would do it."

"What 'it'?" I asked in shock.

"Sell the house and leave the village, taking his daughter-in-law, his wife, his child, and his grandchildren with him."

"What's not to understand," I said. "There's something called shame in this world. Even on this mountain, something called shame . . ."

"No doubt there is, Teacher. Not only on this mountain, but even in the bear who lives inside a cave on this mountain. But in the city or the village, some people have no shame whatsoever . . ."

"Then why did he run away?" I asked.

"I was going to ask you that question," said Halit. "Since you asked it first, then I'll tell you: fear of death."

"Was his son going to be released soon?"

"No amnesty-shamnesty, he still has ten more years."

"So?"

"Look at us. Carried away in the story and forgot the stove." Halit said. He got up from the chair he had been perching on, opened the stove lid, and, picking two dung cakes from the pile in the corner, tossed them over the dying embers. Then he reached for the kettle. Frowning at his luck, he said, "We're out of tea, too."

"Then make some more," I said.

As if he were hiding his face from me. He put two pinches of tea in the kettle, poured hot water in it, and let it steep. When he turned toward me, I asked, "Did Ibram's father know you?"

"He did."

"Did he know you and his son were cellmates?"

"He did."

"Then he knew you'd be released soon."

"He sure did."

We both remained silent.

I waited for a dog to bark, a wolf to howl. Or for the moon to rise, to break this darkness a bit. But neither a dog barked, nor a wolf howled, nor the moon rose, nor the wind blew. I got up, opened the window. Like before, no light. I filled my lungs with the crisp outside air. As if I were not here but in the farthest corner of the world. And in the cold of the night, in this pitch-black darkness, someone I didn't know, someone lost, was calling to me, asking me to show him the way. A stranger, in a place with no roads to take, no way to choose, in a fraction of time, in the middle of the night. I closed the window. I had no answers to give. Taking the cup of tea from Halit, I asked, "What are you going to do now?" His hand was shaking. He tried to smile.

"Tonight you're asking me all the questions I'd thought of asking you."

"What can I say? I'm a stranger here. You can't ask me this question. You can't expect me to show you the way."

"I didn't ask anyone else. No one else knows it anyhow."

"How so?" I said. "Ibram knows."

He stopped. With a baffled look, he fixed his eyes on mine. "How so?" he said.

"You know that he knows."

"But we never spoke about this," he stuttered.

"Still, he must have said something to you."

He stopped again. I think he didn't want to speak, lest he give away the secret between them.

Then he couldn't resist.

"Yes, he said, 'By the time I am out, the old man will be dead. A pity.' Yes, that's all he said."

Even before he finished his sentence, the dogs started barking.

"They must have caught the scent of the wolves," Halit said. "I'd better go get the dogs inside. Again I overstayed my welcome, Teacher, forgive me."

"Good night, Halit," I said.

Standing in front of the open door as the wintry gust filled the room, he turned and said, "Aren't you going to ask me something else?"

"Was it also true that Ibram's wife had a child with the old man?"

Halit gestured yes.

I don't know why but I also nodded a few times. Was it because I didn't know what to say, or was I trying to warm up, thaw my body frozen by the winter cold? I wasn't sure.

"Halit," I said, "from now on I will never go hunting with you, and you should never tell me anyone's story again."

## THE HUMAN SMELL

As a strange turn of fate and a fitting farewell to me—after I'd lived through fall and winter in this city—the sky seemed to crack open and the rain began to pour in, mixing with the unending thaw in the mountains, running down the roads that the melting snow turned into mud pools, joining the river, a raging dense mudflow that abandoned its bed and inundated all the fields. Even the drivers of the region who didn't bother to chain their tires during blizzards determined that the rain had made the roads undrivable and spent the day at the coffeehouses, doing nothing other than smoking and drinking tea, listening to each other's disastrous tales of winter, wolves, bears, rain, and floods, stories that they had heard and reheard and memorized. When one finished a story, another began, teacups were refilled, cigarettes rolled. Because I could find no one to play chess with, I pulled out Chekhov's collected stories that I had packed for the road and managed to amaze the shop owner by drinking tea after tea without sugar, as if in competition with the drivers. They were usually surprised to see someone who wasn't one of them who could drink steeped tea nonstop, or could shoot and hit, or recognize a purebred horse by its eye or mane, or, better yet, mount that horse and, digging his spurs into the beast's belly, ride it at a full gallop. But they also feel a certain admiration for the stranger who downs ten cups of tea in a row, hits when he shoots, and knows as much about horses as they do.

The shop owner showed this admiration by constantly replenishing my tea, even before I could ask, and never reaching for the sugar jar, seeing that I had not touched the sugar cubes on my table. I drank my tea and enjoyed *The Steppe*, that lovely travel story of Chekhov's, which I had read who knows how many times.

*Among the sedge were flying the three snipe they had seen before, and in their plaintive cries there was a note of alarm and vexation at having been driven away from the stream. The horses were steadily munching and snorting. Deniska walked about by them and, trying to appear indifferent to the cucumbers, pies, and eggs that the gentry were eating, he concentrated himself on the gadflies and horseflies that were fastening upon the horses' backs and bellies; he squashed his victims apathetically, emitting a peculiar, fiendishly triumphant, guttural sound, and when he missed them cleared his throat with an air of vexation and looked after every lucky one that escaped death. "Deniska, where are you? Come and eat," said Kuzmitchov, heaving a deep sigh, a sign that he had had enough.*

*Deniska diffidently approached the mat and picked out five thick and yellow cucumbers (he did not venture to take the smaller and fresher ones), took two hard-boiled eggs that looked dark and were cracked, then irresolutely, as though afraid he might get a blow on his outstretched hand, touched a pie with his finger.*

*"Take them, take them," Kuzmitchov urged him on.*

*Deniska took the pies resolutely, and, moving some distance away, sat down on the grass with his back to the chaise. At once there was such a sound of loud munching that even the horses turned round to look suspiciously at Deniska.*

"That luck of yours, Teacher," the shopkeeper said, interrupting my reading. "After so many snowstorms and blizzards, now the rain."

I closed the book and set it on the table.

"It'll pass," I said.

"*Valla*, even if it passes, the roads must be flooded, hard to reopen."

"We waited an entire winter, we'll wait a couple more days."

"You're right."

The rain slowed down, as if waiting for this exchange to stop.

First it turned to drizzle then stopped abruptly, like it was cut by a knife.

Sümbül Mountain emerged into view, as if washed for the first time since Noah.

Above the pure white summit, a rainbow suddenly appeared, arcing south, as if stretching over all the mountains across the region.

Astonished, the shopkeeper stared at the rainbow that appeared above Sümbül Mountain just when the rain stopped unexpectedly. "God's marvel," he mumbled, "blessed sign."

Soon our bus would be driving under this rainbow.

As I expected, the driver then appeared at the steering wheel and leaned on the horn, calling the passengers.

I got up, reaching into my pocket to pay for all the tea I had drunk, but the shopkeeper refused me, declaring that he wouldn't take money from a teacher who had spent an entire winter in this mountain village.

"You were our guest, Teacher," he said.

That was true. I had been a guest here. I had lived a winter among them and today, on my appointed day, I was leaving.

As I said my thank-yous to the man I wouldn't see again, he said "Don't you worry, Teacher, you'll come again. Sooner or later, these mountains call you back."
After these words, we exchanged blessings and I left. Outside it smelled of mud and damp cow dung. But there was another smell beside this mixture, which I couldn't identify. At first I thought of the damp fleece smell that emanates from the pens, but that wasn't it. Similar, but not the same.
I looked around one more time before getting on the bus. The once empty mud-filled road was now lined with crowds of men and children. I could never understand how they materialized so suddenly, flashing smiles I never entirely grasped and glancing at one another, at the bus, at Sümbül Mountain and the rainbow on its peak.
I also looked one last time at these people, at their postures, their silence, the smiles pasted on their faces, as I got on the bus.

I don't know if I will return here. But I do know that I will never forget this land, the human vistas, the faces in the crowds of men and children lining both sides of the road, their eyes, their lips, all that I will never see anywhere else, until I close my eyes for the last time.

The driver who usually plowed blindly through blizzards was now driving the bus slowly down the incline. The tires slid and swerved as he tried to steady the steering wheel. To our right was a precipice. Down below ran the river: In the summer, naked children and women bathed in its crystal-clear waters, those who knew how fished, those who didn't drowned; the same river that in the winter froze and now had breached its banks and was nothing but a yellow, seething current of mud: the Great Zab.

Chekhov in my hands, I drifted.

*The greasy quilt quivered, and from beneath it appeared a child's curly head on a very thin neck; two black eyes gleamed and stared with curiosity at Yegorushka. Still sighing, Moisey Moisevitch and the Jewess went to the chest of drawers and began talking in Yiddish. Moisey Moisevitch spoke in a low bass undertone, and altogether his talk in Yiddish was like a continual "ghaal-ghaal-ghaal-ghaal...." while his wife answered him in a shrill voice like a turkey-cock's, and the whole effect of her talk was something like "Too-too-too-too!" While they were consulting, another little curly head on a thin neck peeped out of the greasy quilt, then a third, then a fourth.... If Yegorushka had had a fertile imagination he might have imagined that the hundred-headed Hydra was hiding under the quilt.*

I came to as the bus gained speed. We had reached the plateau. The road had not flooded, because it ran above the riverbed.

A little later, we stopped at the Gezne gendarmerie, the first stop we had made on my journey to the mountain village nine months ago. Two gendarmes and a woman spoke with the driver. After voicing his objections, the driver said, "Fine, let her come."

The woman, holding a sack, got on the bus.

She walked toward the back of the bus without making eye contact or talking to anyone.

As she passed by me, she paused and looked at me. Or so I thought. My head was level with her waist.

Then and there, I smelled what I had smelled earlier and couldn't identify when I was leaving the city, but now it lodged itself in my brain indelibly. The new passenger sat in one of the empty seats in the back. Unabashedly, I turned and looked at her.

She looked at me.

Sitting up straight, her sack on her lap, uncertain whether she was eyeing a friend or an enemy, she fixed her gaze at me. I tried to smile but failed.

Facing forward, I took a deep breath.

From my seat, I could smell her smell.

It was the smell of soil, which, after longing for rain as if for years, had suddenly lived through a daylong rainfall and, now satiated, was irrevocably altered.


That was enough dreaming for one trip.

I leaned my sad strange head against the cold window, tried to return to Chekhov's story. But in vain. She was in my mind.

Alone, a sack in hand, coming and going, where from, where to, the poor woman.

As a stranger, it certainly wasn't my place to talk to her. If a local were seated next to me, I could've talked to him, asked him my questions. But the seat next to me was empty, and those getting on the bus along the road seated themselves as far from me as they could, I suppose so as not to bother me.

I closed the book since I couldn't follow what I was reading. (How can someone talking to himself understand what he reads?) "You've changed," I was telling myself, "these mountains have changed you.

"Not just these mountains," I said, "the people, too.

"True," I said, "but not just people, the dogs and the wolves too.

"No doubt," I said, "along with them, the long dark nights, too.

"And our long conversations too," I said.

"I'd call them outpourings," I said.

"Let's call them that," I said.

"Outpourings of the soul, and the bladder, during cold, snowy nights.

"Yes, both, but it's good to add one more: our reading.

"And who knows, maybe our writing as well.

"You know, we didn't write much.

"What about the letters? What about those petitions?

"Those don't count; besides, why are you reminding me of all these?

"Because."

Who was she?

I couldn't hold back. Called the driver's apprentice to ask who the woman was, where she was coming from, where she was going. As if my questions were perfectly natural, the boy said, "An ill-fated one, Teacher. From Piran. Her husband said, 'You're nulled' and divorced her. She is from Muş. She's traveling back there, to her village. She doesn't even have loose change with her."

I turned to look at the back seats. Then, closing my eyes, I took a deep breath.

Arid roads, parched fields, dried-up bushes, grass, shrubs, wild, flowerless, fruitless trees, dreamless sleeps, untouched women, sharpened knives, mountain fires, a fugitive fox, a wounded mountain hare, a hand touching a hand, an elegy, dying children, two elegies, news on the radio, three or four words learned from the letters you received, two or three words you taught, the steamy *yufka* bread brought on a platter, herbed cheese on the side, a young girl's eyes looking into your eyes, a neighing horse, a barking dog, and another, and a third, then the whole pack, then the wolves laying siege to the village, all of them, with all of their colors, their presence and their absence, and the smell of humans burning my throat, here beside me, all of them were coming with me.

*The Steppe*, this story that resembled mine and was different, that lovely, melancholy story of travel, perhaps you will know, ends with the question: "What would that life be like?"

# HAPPINESS

I WAS ASSIGNED to a mountain village as the director of housing. The project I had proposed based on expert surveyors' reports had been approved by the Ministry and I was appointed as the sole administrator and supervisor (since not a single administrator or technical staff member had been willing to transfer to such a region, with such an assignment).

Once in this village made of countless (what I'd call) caves big and small, I corroborated the validity of expert reports: The village had no roads, no electricity, and most of the caves where the villagers dwelled were in imminent danger of collapsing.

As my first task, I moved into one of the vacant caves. Relative to the villagers' caves, mine was considerably bigger, more solid, and better ventilated. On its walls were drawings of strange figures, unlike other caves. When I asked the villagers why they had left these caves empty, their reply was: "Those are not ours."
Then whose caves were these?
"Others'."
"Which others?"
They wouldn't answer.

Or shrugging their shoulders, they'd just impart two or three words: "Others, you know, strangers."

The absurdity (or uselessness) of my question was obvious. I made do with noting on my work log that the expert surveyors must have overlooked this fact, or noticed it but dismissed its importance.

I was here as an architect, not as a surveyor or an ethnologist. But before too long I realized that my efforts would not be limited to merely getting houses built and moving the people from their caves into those houses.

Before presenting my project to the villagers, I examined how they lived. Then I informed them of the danger facing them. The caves they lived in would soon collapse. But none of them seemed to believe me or worry much about the imminent danger. And when I finally presented my project to these people who lived by hunting or raising livestock, they had no reaction—negative or positive.

Only one person, the oldest among them, asked me, "If you build us new houses, what will become of these caves that our forebears lived in?"

"Well, they'll collapse in any event," I said.

"Then why aren't you repairing them?" the elderly man asked.

I explained to them that the new houses we would be building together would be more sanitary for them; that if the new houses were built, new roads would be built; and, who knows, they might even get electricity in the village. They understood none of it.

Or they understood everything too well.

The elderly man said, "Then the strangers would move here, and we couldn't handle them."

Which strangers?

Who?

Why would they move here?

Why would it be necessary to handle them?

I knew that my questions would remain unanswered.

The only answer I received was: "This here is God's mountain, God's lands. You can build whatever kind of house you want. And we wouldn't stand in the way."

"But we'll build those houses for you, and if not for you, if we don't work together, I wouldn't be able to build anything," I said.

"We wouldn't build houses we don't know whether or not we'll live in, and we can't help you on this matter."

*Nothing to do*—that's what I wrote in my work log. I gathered all my project drawings and returned to my cave. I had to leave them in their soon-to-crumble caves and return to my office and my family. Yet I don't know why but I couldn't.

I must have failed to adequately explain to them the danger they were facing. No doubt, I hadn't used the right words to describe the opportunity of the new lifestyle we were offering them.

And to succeed, I decided to disregard the job I had been given. Rather than building new houses, I chose to repair the caves they were living in. And what's more, to do so, I willingly engaged in deception by using the budget the Ministry had approved for new construction. Hauling sand and cement on muleback from the city, enlisting the help of the villagers, we repaired the caves one by one.

The inhospitable villagers didn't know how to thank a stranger either. But they worked tooth and nail to do everything I asked of them.

All the repairs took us six months. And maybe a bit longer. Throughout, I lived in my cave, just like them. I didn't draw a single sketch during those six months. Didn't even use one of the house plans I had brought along, not even for myself.

I wrote fake progress reports to the Ministry as if I were completing the process.

And once the repairs were completed, I did not return to my office and my family as I said I wanted to. (The reason behind my decision was perhaps the fear of prosecution on the grounds that I had abused my office, did not build new houses and relocate the villagers into them, and used the money I was assigned to repair caves instead.) I chose to cut my ties with my past life and continue to live here among the people who lived inside the caves.

I no longer counted the days, weeks, months, or years. No one was looking for me, no one asking about me. I had come to this mountain village as an architect but now live as a hunter. My house is a cave that once might have belonged to strangers, its walls covered with paintings.

From time to time, especially at night, as I stare at these wall paintings in the trembling light of a candle, I imagine that the people who once lived in this cave, and their gods whom I didn't know and therefore believe in, are starting to trust me, and, why should I lie, I vaguely sense the wary wingbeats of a feeling that resembles happiness.

*Minimal Tales*

## HORSELESS

I also wanted to escape. But they didn't let me. In the
end I found myself among my captors, rather, those
who themselves couldn't escape.


So you want my permission to leave.
What would I tell the others, if they asked?
But if you're set on leaving, that's another matter.
Let me come with you. Then we'd owe each other
nothing.


No, I've no horse, we can't ride together.
I have a rifle, yes, but no horse.
Besides, if I had a horse, would I until now...

## INTERVIEW

You writing it down? asks the old villager who smells
like damp fleece.
Don't you see I am? Keep talking.
What nonsense!
Shall I write that?
Write this: I got no patience left.
I write, I got no patience left, repeating it.
Not you, it's my patience.
The same thing. What else shall I write?
Isn't that enough?
(I look puzzled; so he says)
Make our photograph, if you want.
(He calls his daughters, sons, grandchildren, his sons'
brides, his wives.)
Here, like this. Make a nice picture, all of us together.
You can include it in your story.
This way, you won't forget us.
Send us the pictures. No need to write us letters.

## THIS

What's this?
Snow.
I've never seen snow like this.
O the things you'll get to see here.
And what are those things?
Wolves, dogs.
What else?
Bears, foxes.
What else?
A human being, if you're lucky.
In this snow?
In this snow, if you can find your way. Or if he's lost
his way. Luck of the draw…

## MY MOTHER AND ME

The village is gone.
(Even) the children are dead.
Of his family, only his mother is left. And him.
That's what he says.
What will you do? I ask, just to have said something.
Unhesitating, he first asks, then answers.
Us? We'll also die soon. Both my mother and me.
Then why aren't you leaving? I ask.
Leave? he says (surprised). We've been everywhere. My
mother and me. Where else is left beside here?

## RUINS

The village is in ruins. Everyone killed, horses, dogs.
These people, aren't they afraid of God? I shouted.
I waited.
My voice did not echo.
My God! What sort of place is this! I added.
What business would God have on this mountaintop?
said a villager whose name I didn't know. He added:
Around here, we settle our affairs among ourselves.
We remained silent.
A dog barked in the distance.

## FORTUNE

The one who stopped me this time was a woman in
ragged clothes. She spoke my language very well.
Stranger, come let me read your fortune, she said.
I smiled. My fortune's been read plenty of times.
But not here, she said. Let me read it here this time.
What do you use, I asked, still smiling.
A mirror, she said.
Then, without waiting for me to respond, she held my
hand and walked me to the poplars by the road. My
hand in her hand, she sat us down.
She pulled a round hand mirror out of her bosom and
held it out.
Look in this mirror, she said. Look intently and try
not to think of anything. Then give it back to me.
I took the mirror that smelled of her sweat and looked.
The mirror was cracked.
I saw my face reflected in the broken, tarnished pieces.
Was this really my face or not, I couldn't tell.
Over, she said and took the mirror back.
Then she inspected the mirror slowly, carefully.
As if the face, the eyes she saw in it weren't hers.
Strange, she said. I see nothing. Either you didn't really
look in the mirror, or you let thoughts cross your mind.
But even your thoughts aren't visible.
You mean my fortune came out empty? I asked.

You shouldn't talk like that. That's the worst kind of bad luck, your fortune coming out empty. Maybe it's me that can't read your fortune.

Or maybe it's because the mirror is cracked, I said.

I've held this mirror in my bosom for years and never once took it out to see myself; it was bound to be broken. But I can't read fortunes with anything but this mirror. Let's try it again, if you want.

She held out the mirror.

I pulled myself up off the ground.

No, I said, I don't want to see my face a second time in a cracked, tarnished mirror.

Then look in my eyes, she said.

I had played this game before.

No, I said. Once is enough for a fortune.

## RECORDKEEPING

What's your job here, I asked.

To record every document received or sent, Mr. Inspector.

And do you read these documents? I asked.

No, sir, he said. My job is only to enter them in the records. No one in our department is tasked with reading documents.

And what are you doing right now?

My apologies, sir, he said (setting his pencil on his desk), I forgot to tell you. I also write down everything spoken around here.

Will you write down our conversation too?

This is what I am doing right now, Mr. Inspector.

But I'm not an inspector.

Doesn't matter, sir. In the East, everyone is responsible for performing their duties. Without asking questions. Without looking to see. Especially without asking or looking to see.

## A CONVERSATION

What are you doing here? asked the watchman holding a rifle who suddenly accosted me.

I'm taking a walk, I said.

Did you get the Bey's permission?

Which Bey? Is there a Bey of these mountains?

There sure is, he said, pointing his rifle toward me. Don't you know the Bey?

No, I don't, I said. I'm in transit here. And now just walking around.

Your ID, please.

What ID? I asked. I'm here for the census. I am a state clerk. If an ID is what you need, here's my ID.

I reached into my inside pocket and took out my official state-issued badge.

This ID is not valid here, he said, without even taking to look at it.

But I'm on duty, I said, I came here to count the people and the animals.

No one counts anything here without the Bey's permission, he said.

Then take me to your Bey, I said.

Our Bey is currently in the capital, he said. But since you traveled all the way here, with or without permission, I can't let you go without offering you something to

eat. It would dishonor our Bey and our customs.
He lowered his rifle. As if to say, Get in front of me,
he pointed the way with its barrel.

# COINCIDENCE

I'd like to rent a boat.

What for? he asked.

I've always enjoyed traveling, I said.

Have you ever killed a captain?

What an absurd question. I'm an honest man, I said.

You may be an honest man. But what you want is more absurd than my question. See here? We're on top of a mountain. No good use for a boat. Anybody misguidedly looking for one around here, if I had to guess, would have to be a fugitive sailor who killed his captain. But if you really want to know, there are barges, not quite like boats but still used for hauling cargo, about 180 kilometers from here, on the Tigris.

Does the Tigris reach the sea? I asked.

So you're not a sailor and you know zero geography. Are you here by mistake?

I must be. Or a coincidence.

As long as you know . . . he started but must have read it in my eyes that I didn't believe him; he walked away without finishing his sentence.

I looked.

It was snowing on the hills.

On the tallest hills.

## THE WATCHMAN

What are you doing here? I asked.
I'm the watchman, he said.
What're you watching? I asked.
I can't tell you, he said.
Why, you don't know it yourself, I said.
You won't get a word out of me, he said.
I'm not trying to, fool. You and me, we're the only living things left around here. Luck of the draw. Just you and me and no one else. Get this in your head and when your watch is over (I hope you know when your watch is over), come find me so we can hit the road together.
I pointed at the ammunition depot ahead: I'll be there. But you should know that I won't be able to wait too long.

## COMPASS/LESS

Compass in hand, I ask, Where are we headed, Ramazan?
The village.
But that's not the village road.
The village has no road anymore, Teacher. Buried in snow. There's no village road until summer.
Then how do we get there?
By forging a new road. What we're doing right now.
But you're forging it in the wrong direction.
Don't mind the compass, Teacher, just follow me.
But you're headed the wrong way, Ramazan.
Then leave me, follow the compass. Forge your own road yourself.

## DARK DREADFUL WINTER

What a snow, Halit!
You haven't seen the worst of it, Teacher, this is still spring.
Spring? A spring winter?
Whatever you say.
I can't see a thing, Halit, whatalotta spring snow this is!
It'll clear out soon, Teacher.
Soon?
Then the wolves descend. Then it's winter again, dark dreadful winter.
What do we do then?
Then we turn inward, Teacher.

## VOICE

Who died, asked a voice.
Who killed, asked another voice.
How many dead, asked a third voice.
When did they kill, asked an unfamiliar voice.
The killers will also die, said a familiar voice.
Three were children, said a different voice.
And five women, said the same voice.
Where are we headed? asked an old voice.
Like you don't know, said a young voice.
He sure doesn't, said the dying voice.
Because with him, the mountain summit he beheld
before closing his eyes also died the window of the
house also died the barking dog also died the water
from the fountain also died the poplar swaying in the
wind also died the melting snow also died and last the
sun died.

## WHO

No cure for him who sees these mountains, an old man once said.

I had taken it as the ravings of old age.

Years passed.

I returned to the mountains.

There were no villages left, not even barking dogs.

I asked the first human I met.

Where did all the people go?

He stared at me vacantly.

My guide translated my question. And the other (thankfully) opened his mouth, uttered a few words. Then, as if our encounter was nothing unusual, he continued walking.

What did he say, I asked my guide.

They went where you came from.

# WELCOME

Good to see you, the young man says, taking my suit-
cases as I get off the bus.
Good to see you, I reply, puzzled.
We've been waiting for you a long time, he says.
He's walking, my suitcases in his hands.
The trip was long, I say.
Don't we know it? he says.
We stop in front of the hotel.
I can't go inside, he says. Get a good night's sleep and
I'll find you here in the morning.
What are we going to do? I ask.
He smiles.
We've a lot to do. Wait till tomorrow.


Morning comes.
He is in front of the door.
Did you sleep well?
I did, I say.
Let's go now and have breakfast, he says.
Breakfast: hot steaming pita, herbed cheese, endless
cups of tea.
What now? I ask.
Now? he says. I don't know. If you want, we can take
a walk in the mountains. You can hunt and I'll watch,

if you want. (He pauses briefly, then adds) If you're ready, I'll take you to them, he says.

Them? I ask.

Yes, haven't you been waiting?

For whom? I ask.

The mountains, he says, laughing.

Then adds: These mountains God also made.

All of us, I say. You, me, all of us.

Noo, he says, not us. Don't joke.

Then who?

These steep mountains, these soilless mountains, these treeless mountains, he says.

But he didn't make humans? I ask.

No, he says. Humans made themselves.

## KEREM

Will I also die before I grow up? Kerem asked.
Why would you die? I said.
Everyone's dying, he said. Night comes and everyone
dies.
Nothing will happen to you, I said.
Then take me along, he said. When I'm with you, you'd
be safe too.
But what about your mom, your dad, your siblings,
your sheep, your dogs?
They'll all die, he said. They'll all die anyway. Let me
come with you. You save me. And I'll save you.

## WHAT

What are you looking for on that ungodly mountain?
asked a familiar voice.
I'm not looking for anything.
I'm just there, on the mountain.
Among its living and the dead. That's all.
That's what I said.
Don't speak like you're one of them. You, why are you
there?
I don't know, I said. Maybe because I'm no longer one
of you but one of them.

# AFTERWORD

> I think we ought to read only the kind of books that wound or
> stab us.... A book must be the ax for the frozen sea within us.
>
> —Franz Kafka

> My writing is something like salting the wound.
>
> —Ferit Edgü

FERIT Edgü often mentions that he was "reborn in Hakkari," refer-
ring to his nine-month stay in Pirkanis, a mountain village in Turkey's
southeastern border province, as the most transformative event in
his writing life. In 1963, just three months after completing his fine
arts and philosophy studies in France, Edgü, then twenty-four, was
assigned to a teaching post in the remote province—a civilian service
alternative to military service for university graduates. For someone
born and raised in Istanbul, the post might as well have been in an
utterly unknown country that, as the Turkish saying goes, "even God
forgot." Edgü's journey would take him to the opposite end of the
country, from the most developed urban northeast to the least developed and most forbidding landscape of the southeast. To arrive in
the municipal seat of the Hakkari Province, Edgü had to cover the
last stretch on foot across a snow-covered mountain. An old sheep-
herder who'd served as his guide out of the city loaned him a horse
to ride the remaining distance over treacherous terrain obscured by
snow. When Edgü pointed out that he didn't even know where the
village was, the old man replied, "Don't worry; the horse knows."

This account, eerily reminiscent of Kafka's parables, encapsulates the existential displacement and isolation that characterize much of Edgü's writing, but these traits gain a new valence in his narratives about Hakkari, including the novels *Noone* and *A Season in Hakkari*, and the stories in this volume, *Eastern Tales* and *The Wounded Age*. At the time of his sojourn, Hakkari, a 2,750-square-mile mountainous province, had a population of barely ten thousand, half of them soldiers, as Edgü notes in the opening of *A Season in Hakkari*. In this new, utterly desolate geography of peaks, deserts, steppes, and precipitous valleys crisscrossed by the Great Zab River, isolation and displacement are no longer the familiar traits of the discontented urban intellectual. Rather, they assume a *material* presence—stark, palpable, inescapable. The imposing landscape is scarred by chronic violence, including the internecine wars of the twentieth century and current subjugation campaigns against ethnic communities, especially the Kurds, whose cultural autonomy remains anathema to the nationalist state. Governed by strife and survival, life in this new reality seems to depend on visceral instinct, on jagged intelligence honed by the unrelenting antagonism of nature and the state, on resilience steeled, paradoxically, by stoic fatalism ("God gives, God takes away," they say).

Edgü likens the narrator of *A Season in Hakkari* to a shipwrecked captain who finds himself "not on a shore but far away from any sea, worse yet, on a mountaintop (elevation: 2.1 km)," and cautions readers that, if they have never experienced a shipwreck, they "may find it difficult to understand what's written in this book.... Because to understand necessitates a common language. And a common language means a common life, a common knowledge, a common background, a common dream, which in some places is a common downfall." Here, no amount of received knowledge, education, or artistic skill proves useful; surrounded by people whose culture is utterly strange to him, Edgü becomes a stranger to himself, too. The titles of the first two books he writes after his return capture the essence of this self-alienation: *Noone*, and even more poignantly, *O*, the original title of *A Season in Hakkari*, which is the third-person pronoun in Turkish. Not merely an observer, he becomes a dispossessed object of observation, just as unfamiliar as the rest of the terrain. These two books as well as *The Wounded Age* and *Eastern Tales* feature abrupt shifts in point of view, disembodied voices, and a near-complete absence of characterization, as if the consciousness behind the narratives has been besieged by its experiences. Not so much an interpreting subject, he is, on the one hand, a transparent conduit and, on the other, an aggregate of experiences as new and formative as those of one "reborn."

The present volume represents the range and dynamics of Edgü's signature style as it has evolved over the course of sixty years and some thirty books of fiction and poetry. Although *Eastern Tales* was published before *The Wounded Age*, their reversed order in this volume is aimed at foregrounding the trajectory of stylistic distillation that characterizes Edgü's writing.

> I want nothing superfluous in my writing. Texts cleansed of details; the event giving rise to the story distilled to its concisest form.... I've tried to do away with narration, fictionalization, similes and metaphors.... I cannot stand metaphorization ... [or] descriptions built with ornate words, long, unbearable sentences that serve as signs of an author's mastery.... Just as we have freed writing from psychology, we must free it from metaphors and similes (nothing resembles anything else).

Indeed, Edgü's stories are "elemental," without extraneous exposition, relying instead on voice, point of view, and tone to convey narrative energy, to express as much as possible in the sparest of styles. His texts are proto–prose poems or flash fiction, or, as the Turkish critic Hasan Uygun has provocatively called them, photobiography— maps of personal memory captured by freeze-frame photography. An accomplished painter and photographer himself, Edgü indeed attempts to bring his language as close to painting or photography as possible. The more austere the language, unmediated by figurative devices, the more evocative and emphatic the words themselves become. Even the local and historical particularities gain an almost archetypal resonance, reflecting the human condition when caught in chronic warfare.

Edgü's style is an expression less of trust than of distrust in the power of words in a world where rhetoric constantly threatens poetry and truth-telling. Reading these spare narratives spurs self-interrogation. The less we are given, the more we want to imagine, and the more we imagine, the less we trust what we think we know. Standing starkly before us, Edgü's narratives remind us—those long inoculated by the self-serving rhetoric and nationalist myths of the state—how little we know about these stories, about the actual human toll of their history.

*The Wounded Age* and *Eastern Tales* were written during an especially tragic period (the 1990s through the early 2000s) in the history of Turkish-Kurdish conflict, marked by incessant clashes between the Turkish military and Kurdish autonomists, the destruction of thousands of villages, forty thousand dead and at least as many people in the southeast forcibly displaced. In other words, these two books chronicle Edgü's memories of Hakkari through the magnifying lens of recurrent history. To use a metaphor (despite the author's admonishment), we can characterize *The Wounded Age* and *Eastern Tales* as "vivisection": looking into an open, unhealing wound. Writing demands a reckoning between memory and actual experience—past and present. Over time, experience is subsumed inside an ever-widening network of memories, associations, fictions, personal or historical narratives of self-valorization, or, for that matter, inside the enduring sameness of the cycles of violence, futility, and loss. Edgü aims not to memorialize events in a closed past but to re-instance their experience as it persists, to re-instance that which is still living. *Ansımak*, a neologism by Edgü, describes this pursuit. In Turkish the verb *anımsamak* means "to recall a memory" or "to remember," and the -*m* and -*sa* verb suffixes following *anı* ("memory") emphasize the subject who is remembering. In Edgü's rendering, *ansımak*, the subject is noticeably absent, and the emphasis shifts instead to the "instance" (*an*), so that the verb comes to mean the re-instancing of experience.

Translating Edgü feels deceptively easy. His vernacular register, the near-photographic neutrality of his narrators, the terse and straight-forward syntax, all seem to promise an effortless translation. Yet re-creating this simplicity has itself required a discipline and restraint on my part. The minimalist stylist who shuns an interpreting subjectivity in his narrator also calls for a translator who must remain, if not altogether invisible, at least inconspicuous, unintrusive. This expectation certainly informed my language strategies, but it also necessitated a degree of self-estrangement on my part. Like *A Season in Hakkari*—which I first read during high school—*Eastern Tales* and *The Wounded Age* coincide with the most formative years of my life, a period of great tumult in Turkey, punctuated by two military coups and the nearly uninterrupted campaigns in the southeast. Returning to Edgü's narratives inevitably stirred up in me old questions, remorse, even shame and anger that could not be allowed to spill over into my translation. To rein in my subjectivity, I decided to complete a full working draft in one month—certainly a first for me—to meet the language on the page, so to speak, as if reproducing a photographic image, attending to the lines rather than the emotional effect of the subject. The result, I hope, is a language that is as austere, unmediated, and crystalline as Edgü's Turkish.

The dissimilar grammar and syntax of English and Turkish, especially acute in the polysemic vernacular forms of the two languages, necessitate that the translator exercise certain creative interventions, in search of correspondences between the language of the source text and the aesthetic capacities of English. The halting syntax, grammatical inversions, the sentence lengths, the abundant comma splices found in this translation are my attempts to approximate in English the syntax, conversational language, and natural cadences found in Edgü's original text. The vocabulary is plain and unadorned in order to re-create Edgü's direct speech, his lack of verbal flourish, and the reverberating lyricism of his dialogues. Just as I always want to read Edgü's text out loud, I'd like my translation to tempt readers to do the same. I also replicated some of the local idioms in order to accentuate the Turkish vernacular. In Turkish, when people are resentful, they have a "bitter smile in their eyes"; they speak of extreme snow- or rainfall in the plural, "snows and rains"; they feel deep cold "in the marrow"; when a woman is very close to her due date, her "belly is at her nose"; when taking leave of friends, we say "forgive my wrongs," and they reply "and you mine."

In a similar vein, I did not translate some of the local diction because, after all, *yufka* is not just any flatbread, nor is *poğaça* any breakfast pastry, nor *salep* any drink of hot milk and cinnamon. Foreign words in translation are talismans; following their tracks (especially in the age of the Internet) reveals much more of their cultural richness than any translation can. Lastly, several Kurdish lines appear both in Edgü's original and in the translation. Although their English versions immediately follow in my translation, these few Kurdish lines are retained in deference to the language of the land and the people that Edgü encountered during his time in Hakkari. These utterances also serve as important historical markers: Especially because they are patently unexceptional, these few Kurdish lines are small but meaningful gestures of rebuke in a country that agreed, as a condition for joining the European Union, to allow limited publication and broadcasting in Kurdish only in 2003.

Edgü's *The Wounded Age* and *Eastern Tales* still retain their piercing clarity, even through endless wars and decades after their original publication. It is not true that history repeats itself any more than that humans are mere spectators watching an endlessly looping reel. The fallacy of helplessness implicates us in this tragic repetition.

—ARON AJI

# OTHER NEW YORK REVIEW CLASSICS

*For a complete list of titles, visit www.nyrb.com.*